ODIN'S BANE

THE SELA HELSDATTER SAGA
BOOK THREE

RORI BLEU
ROSIE CHAPEL

First printing: 2023
ISBN: 978-0-6459731-0-5 (eBook)
ISBN: 978-0-6459731-1-2 (Paperback)

Ulfire Pty. Ltd.
P.O. Box 1481
South Perth
WA 6951
Australia

Cover Design: R Norman
Cover Image: Canva/Deposit Photos
Designed in Canva
Internal images: Canva/Deposit Photos.
Created using appropriate licences.

✾ Created with Vellum

A NOTE FROM ROSIE

One of my favourite things about writing is the research which goes into each story, especially anything mythical, historical, or with historical undertones.

Although I studied the Vikings when at uni, this series demanded diving down the deep, deep rabbit hole of sagas and legends, which span centuries and continents.
It was *the* best fun!

Thank you, Rori.

Thank you, also, to my hubby for his endless support and technical wizardary!

ODIN'S BANE

The Sela Helsdatter Saga
Book Three

Rori Bleu

Rosie Chapel

CHAPTER
ONE

The sudden jerk of the vehicle hitting a pothole, jarred Sela into a semi-conscious state. Bleary-eyed, she tried to recall where she was and in whose car.

It could not be her car because that damn idiot, Loki had destroyed it. At the first opportunity, she was going to kick his dumb ass for...

In that instant, clarity pierced the muddle in her mind, and the memory of the battle between Loki and Odin struck Sela between the eyes like a two by four.

For all her courage, despite everything she had endured, this broke her, and she succumbed to a bout of weeping. She would never be able to wreak revenge on her husband because Loki was gone.

She could not connect with him; not in this realm, nor any of the other eight.

He has... Sela tried to bite back the sob... *gone.*

She could not bring herself to say the word *died*, to believe Odin had snatched her love away with that accursed spear.

Tears cascaded down her cheeks like a spring deluge.

Sela tried to steady herself by glaring at the headliner, muttering balefully, and hoping she was in a hearse being dragged back to Helheim, where she belonged.

Nothing matters now.

With all the magic bestowed on her, the one trick no one had bothered to teach her was how to bring somebody back from the...

She had nothing else to live for. They had all won... Odin, Hel, *Freya...*

Suddenly, a small, powerful voice overwhelmed her self-pity, "Momma, **stop.**"

The command banished the last of Sela's lassitude. She looked around the vehicle in bewilderment to see where the voice had come from.

Questions must be answered.

Staring at the front seat, Sela made out the back of the driver's head. The dashboard light cast a halo about the figure who was definitely female.

The woman's dirt encrusted, tangle of hair might mask her face, but Sela had a pretty good idea as to her identity.

Freya!

Disregarding the fact that she was in the backseat of a car currently hurtling along an old country road, Sela grabbed Freya's hair and, with a crazed shriek, pounded her face against the steering wheel.

"You bat-fowling whore. Your treachery killed Loki."

The car careened wildly as Freya struggled to keep it out of the ditch.

Blood poured from the older woman's mouth and nose as Sela continued her assault.

Unable to defend herself, Freya screamed, "Get off me, you lunatic and sit down."

"I'll show you... you... muddy-mottled scullion," Sela spat, cracking Freya's skull against the side window a few times for good measure. "I've lost everything and your meddling head will be the first..."

Through blood-drenched lips, Freya burbled frantically, "Sela, you are going to kill us all."

Unrelenting, Sela paid no attention.

Her grief-stricken rage demanded the witch's annihilation and she was more than happy to oblige.

Once more, the voice exploded in Sela's mind. This time, it wasn't consoling but furious.

*"**Mother, enough.**"*

Sela tumbled backwards at the command. Her eyes widening in shock as they shot to the front passenger seat.

In Sela's anguish, she had completely forgotten the reason this madness had started.

Sela caught the sight of tiny, demonic-like eyes smoldering back at her from the dark windshield. A chill snaked down her spine when she realized they belonged to her daughter, Anna.

Fear overcame fury. She wanted to look away from Anna's tiny red orbs, but was transfixed.

More tears spilled over as abject confusion wove its way into an already tumultuous glut of emotions.

Using this reprieve to her advantage, Freya pulled her car to the side of the road. Blood splattered everywhere as she spun in her seat.

Heedless that murder was illegal in Midgard... Earth... *whatever ridiculous name they had tagged this dump of a realm,* Freya had no qualms about killing this damn harlot once and for all.

The tiny eyes froze her mid-movement. "No more, Freya. Enough damage has been done tonight."

Freya pressed the back of her hand to her gaping mouth, trying to stem the flow of blood. Like an angry child emphasizing its point, she flung droplets at Sela, glowering menacingly.

"Easy for you to say, Anna," Freya griped. "Your face doesn't resemble freshly ground hamburger."

Presuming further conversation with these two was a waste of breath, Freya fumbled with the door, biting her tongue at the bloody indent in her window. She deluded herself into thinking she ought to be grateful it had not shattered.

The last thing I need is to be sitting on millions of glass shards.

She growled at Anna, "If *you* will excuse me, I'm going to see what else that reckless wi... I mean your *mother*... did to my car."

Slamming the door, Freya howled curses into night for being crazy enough to allow Sela into her life. Avowals of excruciating death and destruction followed the blood-soaked goddess from one end of the car to the other.

At the sight of the immaculate paint job, covered in scratches, and dented by whatever Sela had caused her to sideswipe, Freya stomped into the darkness.

The moment Freya disappeared, Sela crawled into the driver's seat.

In her wrath, Freya had left the motor running, and Sela was determined Anna and she would be long gone by the time Freya registered her mistake.

No sooner had she jammed the shifter into drive — *go figure Freya wouldn't be able to understand a manual transmission,* Sela brooded — than the car died.

Facing her daughter, Sela reminded herself that, irrespective of what had just transpired, she was still the infant's mother. Anna was less than two days old, and she, Sela, was in charge.

Rules ought to be established from the outset, and there was absolutely no way Sela was going to allow her child to call the shots, even if she *did* possess the power to destroy Odin, and control Freya like a puppet.

"Anna, stop playing games. We need to get out of here before Freya comes back with the entire valkyrie army."

"No, Momma. We aren't going anywhere until Freya pulls herself together and gets back here," Anna was adamant.

"I'm your mother, sweetheart, and you will do as *I* say," Sela hoped she sounded more convincing than she felt, given she was carrying on a debate with a baby who, by rights, should not know a single word, never mind be conversing in complete and coherent sentences.

"That... bi... woman is responsible for your father's death. I'll be damned if we sit here and wait for her."

"We need her, Momma. I know that's hard for you to understand, and I don't blame you, but if we don't stay together, none of us will see the sunrise."

Sela had to give Anna credit for inheriting her father's flair for the dramatic, as well as his sarcastic sense of humor when she added, "Besides, do you think winning an argument with a newborn makes any sense?"

Slouching in the seat, Sela crossed her arms, huffing, "I have serious doubts how *newborn* the soul within your body is, but I don't have much choice, do I? Do not think this will go unpunished, *my* daughter."

Anna flashed her mother a gummy smile.

She could see why her father had loved this woman and

bestowed on her the gift of Anna's birth. Anna knew what the future held for the two of them but, however much she wanted to, could not impart a single solitary detail.

Not yet.

The driver's door was yanked open, triggering the overhead light.

While they had a good idea who the intruder was, Sela and Anna squinted into the darkness.

Seeing the outline of a figure bathed in the weak glow, Sela reached for the dagger in her boot, half-expecting a sword to slice her in half before she could grasp it.

Fortunately, that did not happen.

Instead, a hand smacked her temple, accompanied by, "Shift, Sela. You've already done enough damage to my car."

Sela inched across, bumping into the car seat neither Loki nor she had the forethought to bring.

Galled, Sela pondered the possibility, Freya might be a capable parent; dispelling the ridiculous notion when a more plausible explanation presented itself.

Had to be Anna who reminded Freya. There's no way the crackbrained goddess had the common sense to figure it out on her own.

Freya did not make eye contact with either of her fellow travelers as she climbed into the car.

She wanted to dump the pair at the first motel they passed, and ride off into the sunset... unencumbered, but something told her that was *not* in the cards.

The car fired up the instant she turned the key.

The growl of the engine exacerbated Sela's indignation, but she kept it to herself, simultaneously acknowledging the impossibility, considering the other occupants of the vehicle could read minds.

That made her smile... just a little.

With a cough and sputter from the abuse sustained since Freya had gunned it out of the national park, the Cougar sped off into the night... and their destiny.

TWO

Tension hung over the trio like a wet blanket.

In a car full of deities capable of mass devastation at the drop of a hat, no one wanted to be the first to utter the wrong word.

Silence, it seemed, was the wisest of defenses as they drove west.

Grudgingly, and in an effort to defuse some of the strain, Sela had agreed to sit in the back.

In fairness, it was no fun squeezed between the bucket seats being nudged by Freya's boney elbow — something she was *not* prepared to admit.

Settling against the comfortable leather, Sela smiled innocently, shrugging an apology for *accidentally* kicking Freya as she climbed through.

Shit happens, even to goddesses who act like spoiled brats.

Sela scowled at Freya, the impulse to remove the older woman's head, only marginally outweighed by the desire for an explanation. The more Sela deliberated over their situation, the angrier she grew.

Eventually, recognizing Freya was not disposed to talk,

she huffed an aggrieved sigh — which did not go unheard by the driver — and turned her attention to the scenery passing her window in a gray, pre-dawn blur, losing herself in thought... and grief.

Freya stared at the oncoming road, irked she had risked her own neck for the ungrateful wretch in the back seat, cursing herself inwardly.

If I had just minded my own business, there would not be a price on my head, and I could do as I pleased.

She glanced in the rearview mirror, recognizing sadness and desperation in Sela's face.

Recalling the animosity, she had directed at the Midgardian, Freya experienced a twinge of shame.

Sela has just lost the love of her life and the father of her child, her hysterical assault was not unpredictable.

She was not the only one mourning.

Freya's heart cracked. While accepting she had lost Loki as a bedmate the moment he met Sela, he had remained Freya's closest friend and protector.

Now he was gone.

A tear trickled down Freya's cheek, brushed away before anyone noticed.

She hunched over the wheel, spewing worthless death spells at Odin as she drove.

It was futile but made her feel less desolate.

The awkward silence persisted, even when they stopped to swap seats.

Freya had no desire for Sela to touch her precious Cougar *ever* again, but she was exhausted, and even goddesses need their beauty sleep. The moment she sank onto the soft leather, she was out.

Sela wanted to ask where the hell they were bound, but it was obvious she was not going to get an answer out of Freya.

Why do I care anyway? It's only a matter of time before the valkyries track us down, Sela thought gloomily as she considered their next move — blissfully unopposed.

Tired of weaving her way along interminable back roads, Sela pointed the car towards the Trans-Canada Highway.

With all the traffic, there's less chance of being ambushed; too many collateral witnesses for Odin to contend with, I hope.

Her gaze drifted to her daughter, fast asleep in her car seat.

To outward appearances, Anna was an angelic and helpless cherub. A wry grin tugged at Sela's lips at how easily appearances deceive.

It had taken the joint power of Freya and Sela to cast a concealment spell which, at best, only muted the radiant strength of this slumbering newborn's magic. The fact those hunting them had not detected Anna's power was beyond Sela.

Unable to help it, Sela studied her daughter's features, seeing his face in hers. The more she stared, the more she saw Loki.

Loki...

You should be here, with us. You should be leading us to safety right now, instead of Freya and me making it up as we go. Who is going to train your daughter? Frey—

Screeching brakes and a blaring car horn jolted Sela's attention to the road. She slewed back into the correct lane.

Looking over her shoulder, Sela was relieved to note her

lapse in concentration had not disturbed Freya, spotting the crude gesticulation of the passing driver.

A low chuckle broke the quiet.

On any other occasion, her response would be to turn the car around, chase the man down, and cut off his finger as a war trophy but, this time, it was her fault.

"You know, Mother, if you want to kill us, I am happy to contact Odin. I'm sure he'd be overjoyed to oblige," Anna murmured, her eyes still closed.

Sela ignored the snide comment, mildly concerned Anna could reach out to Odin on a whim and expose them all.

Damn you, Loki, why couldn't you leave me with a daughter whose biggest threat was a dirty diaper.

"It's not all his fault, you are just as much to blame for the way I am," she heard from the adjacent seat.

"Would you two mind shutting up?" an irritated voice interrupted the exchange.

The strain had become too much for Sela to handle. Unutterably sad, tired, scared, and haunted by an, as yet, unnamed dread, she snapped, "Please, my beloved child, grant me the privacy of my own thoughts and stop intruding."

Momentarily, Anna contemplated defending her actions but could not summon up the will, already aware of what her mother would say.

Miffed at being ordered about, and deeming the conversation pointless, she wriggled in her baby seat and dozed off.

Furious a mere infant had tuned her out, Sela directed her irritation at Freya.

Her eyes blazed in the mirror, shooting daggers at the cause of her misery,

"And why *are* you still here?"

Although Freya's lids were closed, she was anything but asleep, "*Excuse* me?

Trying to maintain focus on the road, Sela groused caustically, "Was I not clear? Let me repeat my question. Why are you still in this car?"

"You mean why am I in *my* car?" Freya countered, dryly.

"You know damn well what I mean. You could be anywhere in this world... or any world for that matter, but noooo... here you are. If you had stayed out of this all together, and stuck to your cushy existence in Fólkvangr... Loki... Loki would still be alive..."

Sela's words trembled with resentment and pain as she castigated the goddess.

"And you would be dead." Freya let that sink in. "Nevertheless, you are correct, Sela. I did screw up by getting involved but, in the same way destiny... or fate or whatever she's called these days... led you here, Anna forced my hand."

"*Anna* forced your hand?" Sela's stupefied gaze swung between Freya and her tiny daughter.

"Yes, Anna and, given a choice, I might well have let you die to keep Loki for myself, but we both know he would never recover from losing you. A distraught and grieving Loki would be far more devastating than an alive you.

"As for my *cushy existence in Fólkvangr,* I'll have you know, my life is quite the opposite.

"Odin has lost his mind, and why? Your daughter, that's why... a story for another day," she added before Sela could interrupt. "His judgment, his behavior is deluded, irrational, and incomprehensible. He murdered Hodor for making the same battle decision as would have any commander.

"As for my personal happiness, let's just say Loki was not the only one from whom I had to walk away... you know what... it doesn't matter. All you care about is yourself."

Freya paused to rein in some of her outrage and distress over the loss of Hodor. She had never slept with him — not for lack of trying, but his heart had always belonged to Svipul — however, she had the greatest respect for his military prowess.

Striving to control her emotions, she said tightly, "He banished the valkyrie twins, Fate and Destruction, to somewhere even he doesn't know because Svipul possessed the courage to avenge the man she loved, and Herja tried to save her sister, an act of valor for which Odin took her eyes.

"So, no, I am no safer in any place in the worlds than I am in *my* car. At least here, I might actually be of help, more than just saving your pathetic life."

Their eyes met in the mirror, and Freya gave a resigned shrug. "If you prefer me gone, just drop me off and steal my car."

Freya fell silent, crushed by the weight of everything she had lost.

Not ready to forgive, Sela fumed, "Looks like the old man can't control his women anymore. Who'd have guessed feminism would reach Valhalla."

The smashed window caught the corner of her eye; the outline of Freya's head etched in blood on the glass.

Slowly, Sela swung her gaze back to the mirror, stunned when she saw Freya was crying. An emotional response to which she never imagined the goddess would succumb.

Another first in forty-eight hours of firsts, but one Sela struggled to come to terms with.

Goddesses do not weep. They do not fall victim to human

frailties. They are supposed to be the impregnable foundations upon which mortals depend.

Guilt swamped her when she realized, during this horrendous debacle, she had thought only of herself and her own torment.

About Freya's feelings, she had not given a single damn. Pulling to the side of the road, she parked the car.

Sobbing uncontrollably, Freya did not notice either the car stopping, or Sela clambering into the back, startled when she was drawn into a tight hug. She clung to Sela and they wept.

In vain, Sela searched for the right words to acknowledge what this deity had risked to keep watch over her and protect her family, but it was useless.

She whispered, "I'm so sorry, Freya."

It sounded inadequate, but it was all she had.

Eventually, their tears ran out to be supplanted by exhaustion.

Stress and lack of sleep took its toll as the pair dozed off, finding comfort in each other's arms.

THREE

Tap, *Tap, Tap...* the sound started gently from somewhere beyond the horizon in Sela's dream.

*Tap, Tap, **Tap...*** it grew louder as she ventured to the edge of slumber to investigate the source, resolved to put an end to whoever was causing it.

*Tap, **Tap TAP...*** an unidentifiable voice accompanied the noise but Sela, sliding back into oblivion, no longer cared.

TAP, TAP, TAP...

...the insistent rapping refused to stop, prompting a groggy-eyed Sela to reproach, "For goodness' sake, can't a woman take a nap in peace."

Certain she had closed her eyes scant minutes earlier, Sela was irked *anyone* would be so rude as to disturb her.

Instinctively, she raked a hand through her hair, surprised by the bird's nest her fingers encountered, not to mention the odd soggy patch.

Extracting herself from Freya's arms, she scolded, "Can't you ever keep your damn mouth sh—"

"Ma'am, I asked, if everything is ok?" The question, slightly muffled by the glass.

Sela froze when she saw the uniform in the window.

Images of being caught off-guard by the fairies, sharpened her wits. She elbowed Freya in the ribs to wake her.

The goddess batted at her in annoyance until Sela landed a solid jab.

Exasperated with being so rudely awoken, Freya shot Sela a **what?** look.

With studied nonchalance, Sela nodded at the window.

Freya blanched.

"Has your car broken down? It looks like you've hit something, recently, multiple times," the trooper pressed, as he inspected the side of the car. "Do you need a tow? Maybe an ambulance?"

Attempting to compose herself, Sela wondered why that was a cop's first assumption when they saw a car on the side of the road.

Praying she looked vaguely presentable, she plastered on her sweetest smile, and stretched across Freya to wind down the window.

"Why, gracious me no, Officer, we're fine," Sela cooed, in the best American accent she could muster.

She had no clue what prompted it but, for some reason, it seemed like a good idea.

"We just drove until we were plumb tuckered out, and decided to pull over to treat ourselves to a little shut eye."

The trooper gave them the oddest look, tangled together in the backseat. Their beatific smiles, insufficient to ward off his unwanted attention.

Hearts stopped when he stepped to the front door and nodded. "Should I be concerned by either the broken window or the baby in the car seat?"

"Heaven forbid, Officer, not at all," Sela tried to reassure before he asked any more questions, she could not answer, like their destination.

"That precious bundle is my daughter, Anna. She's been such a handful on this trip. She detests long car rides, and when she finally fell asleep..." Sela added an exaggerated eye roll for effect.

Perhaps the trooper has kids and would be sympathetic.

"...we thought it best to make the most of the quiet."

The trooper looked at Sela for a long and agonizing moment, before his shrewd gaze moved to Freya who, sheet white, was grinding her teeth in an effort not to let her smile slip.

Sela squeezed Freya's hand in a calming gesture. She was not sure what Freya intended to do to the cop, but doubted it would end well.

Hoping to alleviate his concerns in order for the man to walk away unscathed, Sela chirped, "As for the window, Officer, the nastiest of big, ol' birds flew smack dab into it. I don't know what kind of birds you have here in Canada, but it nearly scared the wits right out of us."

The trooper scratched his head, weighing up the validity of the broad's crazy story, and whether it was worth pursuing given the paperwork involved.

Nope, it was too late in his shift to deal with this. Whatever **this** *was.*

Sela and Freya were about to breathe sighs of relief when the cop paused at the back corner of the car and swiveled around.

Is he going to run our plate?

Sela was not even sure Freya knew anything about license plates when she had conjured up this beast.

Great, we are going to jail, for sure. Sela just knew it.

The trooper called out, "If you two are done fondling one another, take that piece of shit down the road. I'm not running a bordello on my stretch of highway... and for God's sake, feed that child, she told me she was starving."

Without another word, he climbed into his car and drove off.

The pair blinked at each other before peering over the seat at Anna, who was sitting with her arms crossed, an extremely disgruntled expression on her tiny face.

Sela clambered into the driver's seat as silence descended. Turning on the stereo, she tried to fill the dead air, discovering the static was far preferable to the reception she received from her passengers for her choice of music.

Running out of ideas to keep Freya and Anna entertained, Sela spotted a billboard advertising a truck stop.

An optimistic smile twitched her lips as she considered taking advantage of it.

Couldn't hurt to lag a little bit longer. Besides I'm starving and anything has to be better than this?

Coming to a halt in a parking spot, the Cougar heaved out an ear-rattling backfire. Sela winced as she felt Freya's eyes burn into her back.

Ignoring it, she announced gleefully, "Food."

Hoisting Anna from her seat, Sela was relieved at the prospect of feeding her daughter. It had been way too long since last she had been able to, and her breasts felt as though they were on the verge of bursting.

The waitress had not even handed them their menus, before Sela tucked Anna against her and, preserving her modesty with a thin muslin wrap, let the child nurse.

While Anna staunched her hunger, Sela smiled at the waitress who was hovering.

"Two eggs, over medium please, steak... rare, and coffee, lots of coffee. Hell, just bring a couple of pots."

Freya ordered toast and the waitress went off to give the kitchen the order, returning with two pots of coffee, pouring a cup for each woman.

Despite Sela covering herself, the waitress was unable to mask her contempt at what she considered to be the brazen act of feeding a baby in a diner.

Who does she think she was kidding with that sheet... cling wrap would hide more.

Narrowing her eyes, she spun on her cheap heels and disappeared into the kitchen to voice her opinion.

Her reaction had not escaped Sela. *Way to blow any chance of a tip.*

Freya glanced at Anna, feeding happily, then picked up her coffee. Cradling the cup in both hands, she took a sip, and observed in her best motherly voice, "Maybe, it would be wise not to draw attention to yourself."

Sela drained her first cupful without acknowledging Freya's remark.

Not until she was onto her third, did she respond, "Compared with the two of you, this," she waved her hand at the cloth and her almost hidden breast, "is barely worthy of mention. Didn't we agree... *no* unnecessary magic?

"Between you wanting to explode that trooper in his shoes and Baby Isis here, I'm surprised there isn't a mystical trail bright enough to guide Odin's valkyrie horde to us."

"Don't you dare use that fraud's name in my presence," Freya shot back.

It seemed a fight would spark between these two regardless of the topic of conversation.

"Why shouldn't I? I'm sure she would be immensely more helpful than you."

Incensed, Freya went on the offensive. "Ha, she has no time for peasants, too busy committing incest." Her expression was one of haughty disdain.

Never one to pull her punches, and knowing Isis was not only Osiris's wife, but sister as well, gave Freya a feeling of superiority to the Egyptian deity.

Sela finished her coffee.

The caffeine was sharpening her tongue, wonderfully. She threw out a jagged barb, which was more or less a cheap shot at Freya... and the rest of those who considered themselves above humanity.

"Who are you... or any of those hypocrites calling themselves gods... to be so judgmental of anyone else's culture? You all jump in and out of each other's furs without knowing *who* you are sleeping with."

"That would include your hus—"

"Do not dare besmirch his name. Better yet... just shuddup. I'm tired of being the conduit for you energy vampires."

Freya insisted on getting in the last word. "Vampires, indeed? Everybody knows they're only myths. Now, Bigfoot... there's a monster you should be concerned abo—"

Anna burped softly, then corrected Freya, "Sasquatch, or Yeti, depending on where you are."

Sela switched Anna to her other breast to keep her quiet. A talking two-day old was the last thing they needed.

Freya nodded as she supped her coffee, throwing an obligatory, "Yeah, yeah," at Anna.

"While I have your ear, oh, Great Goddess," Sela's tone bordered on the facetious. "This guessing game as to where on Earth we're going is getting very old, very quickly. I let Loki get away with it and we saw what happened there. Not gonna do it again. Where are you taking us?"

Freya pinned her eyes on the rim of her cup, her gaze following the white ceramic as she lowered it to the table.

Without lifting her head, she answered, "Butte, Montana. Well, to be exact, about fifty miles outside the city limits."

"Why in the name of... *you,* are we going there? Why can't you deities ever choose a spot in the middle of a major city like... oh, I don't know... New York?"

"I have my reasons, Sela, and it's the one place I can guarantee we will be safe," adding almost inaudibly, "That is, if he lets us stay."

Sela choked on her mouthful of coffee, her acute hearing catching what her dining companion had let slip.

Freya was halfway across the restaurant before Sela had a chance to ask her to repeat it.

She watched the goddess pay the bill — no magic or trickery — thinking Freya looked tired and older than usual. Sela had seen that look before, on Loki.

Freya thanked the cashier and left the waitress the change as a tip. Without looking back, she walked outside.

Sela collected herself and, Anna in tow, asked the waitress to bag her stuff to go, that is, if she could *find the time* to do her job.

In a fine huff, the waitress all but threw the food at her.

Even though Anna knew better, she caused the waitress to stumble on her heels, twisting her ankle as she fell. Leaving the woman flat on the floor, howling in pain, mother and child traipsed after Freya.

They found her leaning against the hood of her vehicle.

The memory of an advert for a Sixties classic car popped into Sela's mind, making her grin.

She passed the goddess, who was lost in thought, to strap Anna into her car seat.

Rejoining Freya at the front of the Cougar, the goddess stopped any questions Sela may have had with a curt, "Don't ask. You'll understand when we get there."

Pushing herself off the hood, Sela dug the keys out of her pocket and tossed them to Freya.

"Never thought about it. I respect your privacy. Was only gonna say, it's your turn to drive. You couldn't let me finish my meal could ya... all that delicious food going to waste." Sela slid into the back seat.

Freya chuckled and, making herself comfortable, fired up the car. She glanced into the mirror, preparing to reverse out of the parking spot, spying the Midgardian about to devour the steak.

Winking, Freya teased, "Liar."

FOUR

The ride across the Canadian heartland was one of light, measured conversation, interspersed with an occasional break along the way for gas, food — if the junk they ate could be described as food — and essential bathroom breaks.

Sela was amused that, in this realm, Freya was more or less bound by the rules of human anatomy.

The highlight of the road trip *had* to be the sleazy, no-tell motel they were staying at currently, a result of their resolve *not* to rely on magic.

A fateful decision which, although sensible, had eaten into their rapidly dwindling coin, in turn making gas a precious commodity.

To compound the problem, while the trio had managed to elude the Norse hordes who may or may not be hunting them down, the same could not be said for the United States Border Patrol.

Sela was in a worse predicament now than when Loki and she crossed a week and several lifetimes ago. She had no passport or birth certificate, and now, she had an undocumented child to boot.

On the opposite bed, Freya stared in disbelief at Sela as she explained why.

Arching a brow, the goddess preached, "I'm not even from this overly regulated rock and *I* am smart enough to know I need official documentation."

"Fine, the next time you mythical gods place a bounty on me…"

"*Mythical?*" Freya snorted. "Mind, given the fact, I'm stuck in a fleabag motel with you, my status as goddess is definitely questionable."

"…I'll remember to pack my purse with the proper essentials," Sela spoke over Freya. "Instead of getting all righteously judgy, how about coming up with something helpful to get us back over the border?"

An odd expression appeared on Freya's face, and she was delighted to see Sela wriggle uncomfortably when she asked, "Do you still have those *fjötrum*?"

"*Fjötrum?*" Sela quizzed, cocking an eye at the figure on the other bed, certain Freya was about to do something they both would regret.

"Have you been in New York long enough, the only Norse you recall is expletives?" Freya rolled her eyes.

"Allow me to translate… *fjötrum*… or as you may refer to them in *this* realm… *shackles* and, to be exact, the ones you and Loki stole from my fae when you so rudely tore them to bits."

"*Faen din kjerring,*" Sela growled. "My Norse is fine, thank you very much, and I am well aware what *fjötrum* are. I just want to know, why *you* want them? Loki told me about their special powers."

"Thanks for proving my point… and *damn you, bitch,*

back at ya... but *do* you know where they are?" Freya did not bother to hide her irritation.

"I do. Loki had one set tucked in his belt."

"And the other?" Freya's voice rose a notch. "For crying out loud, Sela, I'm trying to devise a way for us to cross the border, the least you can do is help. Either trust me or we part ways now. *So*, once and for all, where are the other shackles?"

Sela stretched over the bed for her coat. Digging in the inner pocket, she produced the cuffs and dangled them in front of her.

The flickering light from the aged television gave the ancient metal a strange radiance.

Sela suppressed a shudder. "Before I hand over these dangerously magical cuffs, tell me why the fae had them, and why you want them now?"

"Really, you need to know *why* they had them, Sela? *Gods*, even *you* possess the intelligence to figure that one out." Freya's brow shot under her hairline at the ludicrous question.

"As for why *I* want them. To be used in the manner intended originally. I'm going to cuff you and drag you over the border. Regardless of anything else, you have no other choice."

"Hang on one minute. Let me get this straight. We get to the border crossing, with me in cuffs no less, and drive through. Just like that?" Sela scoffed.

Freya nodded on each sentence, and gave a satisfied smirk. "Yeah that about sums it up."

"Aren't you forgetting something?" Sela coiled the shackles in her hand, ambivalent about the merits of this plan.

"Like what?"

"Well, for a start, the fact I'm cuffed for which you have no explanation."

"Oh, already have that taken care of," Freya reassured.

"Am I permitted to ask how?" Sela asked, dubious as to whether handing the cuffs to Freya was in any way sensible.

Rising from the bed, Freya went to her satchel on the desk, and rifled through it like a coupon queen looking for the last voucher for a free can of brown, raisin bread.

Sela watched, tensing slightly when Freya spun to face her, half suspecting to be confronted by a magical weapon.

Freya handed her something infinitely more deadly.

The first page was an arrest warrant for murder and bail jumping, bearing the name Sela Helsdatter in bold print.

The mugshot was hideous.

"Your sorcery must be slipping, witch," Sela berated, mildly affronted. "That is a terrible likeness."

On the second sheet, stamped in red, EXTRADITION APPROVED.

Sela read the charges carefully, which included the alleged flight from justice, then lifted indignant eyes to Freya whose smirk was nothing short of triumphant.

"When did you conjure these up? I thought we agreed, no magic?" Sela was positive Freya did *not* concoct this plan; it was too bizarre.

No way had the goddess garnered a working knowledge of the American legal system.

"Nope, no magic. At least not *recently*." Freya chuckled. "*Procured* these beauties when Anna ordained my presence in this forsaken dump. *I* think I did a spectacular job capturing you as a wanted criminal, even if I do say so myself.

"I'm guessing the New York Police Department would

like to have a conversation with you about Peer's death too."

"Was that your plan all along?" Sela asked, unable to believe what she was hearing.

Sela scanned the documents to ensure there was not a side trip to an NYPD jail cell.

Examining her makeup in the mirror, Freya put Sela's fears to a vaguely uneasy rest. "No, those papers were with the faes. Just in case they were stopped after acquiring the two of you."

"If you arranged this so meticulously, why didn't the stupid fae tell us to save their lives?"

"Would you have gone with them?" Freya arched a brow at her reflection.

"No, probably not," Sela admitted reluctantly.

Freya relieved Sela of the papers. "That's what Anna thought." Her grin smug as she checked everything was in order.

Satisfied, she glanced up from the stack, and asked a rhetorical question. "You don't think I had any part in planning this do you?"

Folding the papers neatly, Freya replaced them in her satchel. Perching against the dusty desktop, she crossed her arms preparing to ward off of the litany of reasons the ploy would fail.

To her surprise, Sela was sitting on the edge of bed staring through the cuffs in her open hands, lost in thought, presumably mulling over the logistics of their subterfuge.

That the younger woman was prepared to accept a plot contrived by an infant rather than one cooked up by a goddess, *did* dent Freya's ego slightly.

Bored with waiting for Sela to respond, Freya decided to

watch whatever was flickering on the television screen. It amazed her how easily these Midgardians were distracted by this mindless box, ignoring the irony when, immediately, she became similarly engrossed.

Mesmerized by a family whose only discernible talent was creating something called a sex video and whoring out their drunken daughters, Freya was jerked back to reality when Sela turned off the set.

"If I agree to return these cuffs, do you swear with your blood, you won't hand me over to Odin to save your own hide?"

Sela's question was harsh, she knew that, but it needed to be asked.

Freya didn't waste time feigning wounded honor. She would be equally suspicious had the roles been reversed.

Drawing Sela into a reassuring hug, keenly aware any other answer would have been met with a healthy dash of skepticism, Freya made good use of the moment by swiping the cuffs.

Relinquishing her embrace, Freya shoved the bulky cuffs in her jeans' pocket.

Twinkling unrepentantly, she switched the television back on, climbed onto the bed, wedged a pillow under her chin and, without taking her attention from the screen, patted the covers.

Chuckling at the goddess's impudence, Sela shook her head, grabbed a pillow and joined Freya on the bed to watch the umpteenth unexpected pregnancy to befall that poor, rich family.

"Has Anna provided a reason for *her* presence in the car?" Sela quizzed, expecting more documentation to materialize out of thin air.

"No, our baby genius neglected to address that part.

Never fear, Momma has it covered," Freya pledged, patting Sela's hand reassuringly as she did, her eyes glued to the flickering screen.

"Now, shut up. These people have bigger problems to worry about. How ever are they going to decide which Jaguar to buy?"

FIVE

S ela woke with serious misgivings regarding the merits of this harebrained scheme, which continued while she stood in the miserable, mold infested motel shower, the details running nonstop through her brain.

Her doubts lingered as she gulped down a cup of tepid, day-old coffee, desperately trying to persuade herself the plan had *any* chance of succeeding.

Before she could talk herself out of it, she was next to Freya's Cougar, her hands secured behind her back, her limited magic draining into the cold steel of the cuffs.

Loki had told her these cuffs were ancient, but they were forged from a metal used in *this* realm for over four millennia, making her ruminate on their actual age.

Extending that thought... if they were crafted prior to two thousand BC, from where did they originate? Leading neatly to the question of which race...

Freya interrupted Sela's train of thought, seizing her by the arm and shoving her in the back seat of the car.

Sela started to harrumph at the rough handling but

stopped in mid *rumph* when she saw how Freya was dressed.

Framed by the opened door, the goddess of sex and sophistication resembled some minor cable channel's bounty-hunter extraordinaire.

Slack jawed with shock, Sela speculated which budget trailer park Freya had frequented. *How else could she have dreamed up that snug, black pleather skirt — which scarcely reached her mid-thighs — and the clingy leopard print top. It leaves nothing to the imagination.*

The longer Sela studied the ensemble, the less concerned she was about the magic Freya must have squandered creating it, and the more that Freya's boobs would explode out of the top if she dared breathe.

Now that would be magical karma.

Saving her criticism of Freya's fashion sense for another day, Sela reverted to lodging protests about police brutality.

The goddess did not want to hear it, and held up her hand like a traffic cop to halt the whining. "One more complaint, Ms. Helsdatter, and I *will* hand you over to the authorities."

Sela fulminated inwardly as the car door slammed shut, furious she had agreed to this... not a hundred percent sure she actually had.

Observing Freya's attempts to inch her tightly-clad body onto the driver's seat, Sela defended herself, "You didn't need to cuff them so tightly... that's all I was gonna say."

"Rubbish, Mother," Anna barked from within the depths of her car seat. "Your mind has been swirling with complaints about this since last night. I've been trying to block you out, but ended up with a migraine. Please Freya, just get her over the border."

Sela bore the brunt of their steely glares, and shut up. Aware they were still tuned into her, she promised they had not heard the last of this.

Their route through Willow Creek to the Canadian Border Services Agency Office was not exactly a tourist drive.

The reason they had selected this particular station was because it boasted one of the lowest number of crossings between the US and Canada, and was only open during tourist season.

An appealing option given it was likely to be understaffed or, at the very least, manned by border agents who were probably not the crème de la crème of their graduating class.

Sela's wrists felt as though they were being chewed by the unforgiving metal, and her fingers were going numb. She had to flex them continually to keep the blood flowing.

She bit her tongue, cognizant any protests about her situation would fall on deaf ears.

The sight of the approaching station made her stiffen in her seat.

Freya slowed to a stop with the confidence of owning the place. A smoldering smile greeted the young guard's arrival at her open window.

"Afternoon, ma'am. Papers, please."

His request was professional but his eyes were drawn to scant material, which struggled to contain the driver's more than ample breasts.

Neither did the skimpy skirt, highlighting her shapely legs, escape his notice.

That she still had the power to entice men after countless eons, made Freya beam inside. She hoped her luck would prevail at their destination.

"Good afternoon, Officer Hunky," Freya flirted, her accent impossible to identify. Considering the way she looked, she hoped the agent wouldn't care. "If you can give me a second, Sugar, I'll get them for ya.

"Looks like I'm gonna hafta dig through this suitcase of a purse." Hoisting her oversized handbag onto her lap, making sure the border agent got an eyeful of her boobs, Freya exaggerated every gesture while seeking the necessary documentation.

Sighing dramatically, she tipped the purse upside down. The contents slithered off her skirt onto the seat as she opened the door and shimmied around to alight the vehicle.

She stepped out. Her legs seemed a mile long, complemented by a pair of black patent stilettos, the silver heels of which could be used in self-defense, should that prove necessary.

If Freya was expending this much magic to pull off the charade — a move Sela remained convinced would get them caught — she was going for broke.

Straightening up, the normally diminutive goddess was eye level with the border agent.

A fact not lost on him, either.

"M-Ma'am," he stammered. "Y-you need to stay in your car."

Instinctively, his hand went to his service pistol, only to drop back to his side.

Ignoring his instruction, Freya bent over. Black lace

panties peeked under the skirt's hem as she continued her search.

Eventually, she *retrieved* her errant passport from the jumbled mess, flashed a smile and a wink over her shoulder. "Found it."

In a fluid move which would have made a gymnast or stripper jealous, Freya unbent and spun around, *unintentionally*, grazing the man's hand with her fingertips when she presented her papers.

"You're a sweetheart, Officer Hunky, for being so patient."

"Mathis, ma'am." The agent blushed.

"'Scuse me, Sweets?" Freya was the epitome of innocence.

"My name, ma'am. It's Mathis, ma'am," the agent reiterated as he checked her passport.

With a broad, seductress-red lipstick smile, Freya giggled coyly. "Why aren't you just a bowlful of sugar, Officer Hunky Mathis."

As Sela watched Freya charm the guard with the finesse of an expert, she understood what men saw in her... what Loki had seen in her.

Casually, Freya brushed against Mathis, noting the goosebumps peppering his neck when her warm breath caressed his ear.

"Now, if you would be a dear and let me be on my way, I have to get my cargo," she cocked a thumb at Sela, "over that there border and to the office before nightfall. This car turns into even more of a pumpkin than it looks right now."

The agent did not want to move from the vivacious woman draping herself all over him, but he had a job to perform.

"The woman in the back seat? Does she have her passport?"

He bent to peer through the window at the woman with the pained expression who was muttering to herself.

"Is she *handcuffed*?" Mathis scrutinized Sela, who was babbling to herself about how much she hated Freya, willing the entire pantheon of Norse deities to strike her dead.

Mathis turned back towards the woman, repeating firmly, "Ma'am, *is* that woman handcuffed?"

Freya remained unfazed by the agent's sudden sense of duty. The smile on her lips never wavered.

With the skill of a magician, she produced the extradition papers out of nowhere, and handed them to Mathis.

Deciding the coquettish approach wasn't working, she switched tactics and addressed him in a more businesslike manner, "It's all perfectly legit, Agent. As you can see, our friend there is wanted for murder in the States.

Freya was trying to maintain her composure, but a slightly nervous, unnecessary story felt the need to trip over her lips as he flipped through the paperwork.

"Evidently, jumping bail and crossing the border was her way of proving her innocence. I'm just here to make sure the people of the fair state of Montana give her the opportunity to do so in court."

Mathis was about to question the legality of the transfer when Freya handed him an official-looking business card from the Minister of Justice's Office, and all but purred, "If you have any questions, please feel free to give this gentleman a call. I'm sure he will be happy to explain the importance of international cooperation between our two sovereign countries, in detail no less."

Mathis pointed at the baby in the front seat. "What about her? I don't see anything in the papers about a baby."

"Collateral damage. Seems our friend in the back was pregnant when she absconded. I can't very well leave a newborn alone in Canada now, can I? Imagine the international sensation that would cause if the press got hold of the story? Not to mention the innumerable reports you'd have the pleasure of completing, in triplicate... before your irate bosses showed you the door."

She let that sink in, adding a forlorn, "If you want to take it..."

"Stop." Mathis's brain was reeling at the pandemonium in which he could end up embroiled. "Kindly get into your vehicle and take it, *as well as yourself*, out of my country."

He stamped the papers and thrust them at Freya.

Before she could thank him, he had stomped into his shack.

"Damn, I wish my magic worked that fast." Freya chuckled in Norse as he vanished.

"Fast? At your age, witch, you're lucky your magic works at all," Sela grouched. "If you will be so kind as to get these off my wrists, please?"

"In due time, my dear." Freya climbed back in her car. "We aren't over the border yet and I have no intention of repeating this little performance for any of the US border patrol."

Shutting her door, gingerly, she griped, "Why is everybody so hateful of my girl? She only needs a little buffing... and a lot less Sela Helsdatter."

"How on earth did you produce a business card for the Canadian Attorney General?" Sela had to know, ignoring Freya's barb.

"Well, you see…" Freya began, to be interrupted by Anna.

"Don't even start, Freya. You know full well you got it from me. If I had left it to you, the agent would have been connected with The Norse Psychic Hotline."

In disbelief, Sela croaked, *"The Norse Psychic Hotline?"*

"Sadly, yes. Our goddess friend here isn't satisfied conjuring up whatever she needs, she has to run a phone scam on the side," Anna tsked at Freya.

"What scam?" Freya chided, "I guarantee every caller gets to talk to a genuine Norse Goddess…"

Sela snorted. "Really? Do you tell them the truth or what they want to hear so you make more coin? You are one of the most powerful beings in existence, yet you can't help swindling the gullible, can you?"

"A woman has to maintain her lifestyle somehow these days, doesn't she?" Freya grinned at the infant cheerfully.

"Now, if either of you has keener psychic skills than I, you already know the mess we are driving into."

CHAPTER
SIX

Sela perched on the trunk of the Cougar, breastfeeding Anna, grateful to be in the middle of nowhere which provided some semblance of privacy. Modesty had become a long-lost luxury.

Made no difference to Anna, content Sela's maternal instincts had kicked in, despite the trauma she had suffered during the birth and in its immediate aftermath.

For all Sela's outward insouciance, Anna knew her mother's love was fierce, profound, and indissoluble. It was all she needed.

While the new mother was busy tending to her daughter's needs, Freya had located the last functioning phone booth in the state of Montana, outside a diner bearing the — predictable, if bereft of flair — name of *FOOD*, southbound on US 87, just outside Loma, Montana.

How she had, remained an enigma, one Sela filed away with all the other mysteries which were quintessentially Freya.

While feeding Anna, Sela twisted herself into shape akin to a pretzel to rub her wrists without dropping her daughter. Both were bruised from the blasted cuffs. Fortunately, the numbness in her fingers was wearing off.

She hoped her meager powers would be restored as quickly as Freya had asserted.

Forgetting her discomfort, Sela admired the splendor of the scenery where the Teton and the Marias Rivers flowed into the mighty Missouri, joining its journey to split the Dakotas in two, before rushing into the Mississippi...

Damn you, television for teaching me that useless tidbit of geographical information, when I would prefer simply to enjoy the view, swearing, once they were safe, she would curb her minor addiction to that cursed box.

Sela dragged her gaze from the spectacular surroundings to her traveling companion.

Speaking of entertainment...

The animated conversation Freya was having on the phone proved a far more interesting distraction. It was evident the person on the other end of the line was *not* receptive to anything she was saying.

Grinning widely, Sela watched Freya gesticulating frantically to emphasize whatever point she was trying to make... all the more humorous given the person at the other end could not see the dramatic pantomime.

Sela's mirth dwindled when Freya smacked her fore head, removed the phone from her ear, and scowled at the handset. Her disgruntled expression accompanied the bang of the receiver being hung up.

Exiting the booth, Freya threw her arms up in disgust and stormed to the car.

In an ancient dialect only she knew, Freya released a string of debilitating curses at whomever she had called. She hopped on the trunk next to Sela and glanced down at Anna, who was still feeding.

"For the last time, cover up when you feed her? If for no other reason that she doesn't need a case of sunburn at four days old, and, for crying out loud, change her diaper."

"It's not like I'm on display. Except you, there's not a single soul around," Sela huffed, but did tweak the soft muslin over her exposed skin.

"Problems?" She made a creditable attempt to sound concerned.

"Maybe yes, maybe no. I'm not sure our welcoming committee is particularly excited to see us." Freya looked crestfallen at the notion.

Sela winked at Freya in an attempt to cheer her up. "What? The goddess of charm is having relationship problems. I know a psychic who might be able..."

"Shut up, and look after your child," Freya snapped, the phone conversation haunting her. "We don't need some sleazy trucker stopping to ask you to add a few drops of milk to his coffee."

Without another word, she hopped off the trunk and, with a flick of her hand, her slutty attire reverted to her preferred jeans and t-shirt.

Stuffing her hands into her pockets, she trudged into the diner, wanting to be alone.

Sela was saddened at Freya's sudden change of emotion, noting, with a frown, the slight aging of her friend's features.

Her beauty had not diminished, but the odd wrinkle was visible at the corner of her eyes which lacked their usual luster.

While, in Sela's opinion, this merely added a depth of character to a flawless face, she appreciated that for a goddess who cherished her looks to the point of vanity — the transformation might be a trifle alarming.

She watched Freya shove open the door, pitying anyone who thwarted her right now.

"Presumably, her previous outfit was either too slutty, or not slutty enough to win over whoever she just called, not to mention with that little display, it's as though she doesn't care if we get caught," she mused to her daughter who, wisely, kept her counsel.

She put Freya's emotional baggage out of her mind to tend to Anna.

Laying the infant on an old blanket folded on the trunk of the car to protect delicate flesh from the accumulated heat in the unforgiving metal, Sela removed the diaper, trying not to retch.

"Good grief, girl, couldn't you magic this away? Honestly, you're worse than your father, and that takes some doing."

"No magic was *your* rule. I'm being very good and doing as I'm told," Anna said sweetly.

"You wait until you're old enough for me to train you in swordsmanship. I'm so gonna remember this day," Sela vowed.

She finished changing the apple of her eye, scooped her up, stowed everything in the trunk, and followed Freya.

The smell of stale, greasy food permeating the diner, threatened Sela's gag reflexes more than anything Anna could produce. She swallowed hard, and scanned the interior, spying Freya sitting at the counter nursing a cup of coffee.

Perching on the adjacent stool, Sela asked the waitress to bring her a cup and freshen up Freya's.

Pre-occupied, Freya didn't acknowledge the gesture.

Nudging her, Sela smiled and whispered, "There's a

word these people use when somebody does something nice for them. Let me see... what is it? Oh, yeah... thanks."

Taking a swig of the warmed swill, Freya said absently, "You know Loki meant the world to me, too."

Startled, Sela gaped at Freya, confused and hurt. "Why would you—"

Freya took another drink, "He did and, at one time, I would have given him my very soul. I certainly tried to."

Freya fell silent for a second. She hated feeling vulnerable, especially in front of the woman to whom she had lost Loki.

Sela's gaze lowered to her mug, desperately trying to understand why Freya was deliberately causing her more sorrow. Aggrieved, she shoved the cup away and got down from the stool, halting when Freya grasped her hand.

"Please, I want you... I need you... to understand that, Sela. I took myself out of the equation because I knew we could never be and it was agony seeing you two together, seeing your love, your happiness. I'm so sorry if you ever doubted your husband's devotion."

Giving Sela's hand a light squeeze, Freya gulped the dregs of her coffee, studying the grounds as though trying to read them.

Remorse swamped Sela as she recalled waking alone in bed when this shit with Odin started and immediately blaming Freya for Loki's absence. For the ease with which she attributed every problem that arose between Loki and herself to Freya.

Quietly, she settled back on the stool.

Looping her free arm around her... friend — inwardly dumbstruck to realize the appellation was the truth — Sela hugged Freya.

Brushing Freya's cheek with a sisterly kiss, she whispered, "Who was on the phone?"

Freya stared blankly across the counter. Her pain was palpable, "A ghost who can't... oh, Sela... why do I always screw up everybody's lives?"

She was pale and trembling.

Sela drew her as close as possible without dropping Anna, and soothed, "You don't, hon. How many times have you saved me from Death's door."

Trying to elicit the smallest of a smile, she added, "You gotta know how hard it is for me to admit that."

"Yet, in my wake, I've left a succession of broken hearts and lost souls," Freya brooded, sliding the empty cup across the counter, nearly sending it over the edge.

"Ancient history, love," Sela consoled.

"Not as ancient as one could hope," came the considered response.

Freya tossed money on the counter and traipsed out of the diner.

Sela grumbled under her breath of how she was beginning to hate these food breaks. Inexplicably they brought out the worst in both of them.

Gulping the rest of her coffee, she chased after Freya.

"One day, you're going to take me to a restaurant for a nice dinner, and actually let me enjoy it," Sela decreed as she strapped Anna into her car seat. "I'm talking about an enormous steak dinner with all the fixings... *and* dessert."

"You'll get fat," Freya sallied in a weak attempt at humor.

"I doubt it. I'll just catch up on the calories you keep denying me on this trip," Sela refuted, chuckling wryly.

Claiming her spot in the back seat, she pricked up her ears when Freya tossed out, offhandedly, "If that's what you want, I know a small steakhouse outside Butte which serves the best food this side of the Mississippi.

"The owner is a bit grisly, but I can guarantee the steaks aren't," Freya sounded like a television commercial.

The engine fired to life, preparing to convey its passengers the final two hundred miles to Butte, a three-hour journey which Freya hoped would be long enough to invent a good reason why *he* ought to forgive her rather than grind her into one of his burgers.

She knew his temper... but she also knew his passion for her, or *used to have* for her.

Freya prayed there was something left of his heart... that she had not destroyed it completely.

The closer US 87 took the Cougar to Interstate 15, the more Freya's anxiety about their reception in Butte heightened. She had no idea how to atone for the pain and embarrassment she must have caused him when she disappeared without explanation.

Not helped by Sela kicking the back of her seat like a spoiled brat, whining about the boring, hour-long drive to Great Falls and how it was the worst part of the whole trip.

Keenly aware that the road from Loma was monotonously straight, Freya had prayed for a surprise attack from the valkyrie horde, just for something to do, and to shut Sela up.

Her companion's cheers any time they came to even the slightest deviation in the road was the last straw.

"Don't make me stop this car because I shall."

Freya did not even know where the words came from or what possessed her to say them, but they made her fellow travelers roar with laughter.

Sela's singsong, "But, Mom..." and cheeky grin, pulled a

responding smile from Freya, who added, "Don't say I haven't warned you."

The mood among the trio lightened when they reached Great Falls and the Interstate. Before long, they were on the outskirts of Butte.

Of all the places Freya could choose to hide them, Butte Montana would not have been on Sela's list.

It was a nice enough town — a relative concept in the sense that it was home to more people than any other place they had seen since entering the state — but it was not New York, and she was not returning to their apartment with Loki and their daughter.

That chapter of her life had been unceremoniously slammed closed.

She scarcely registered the historic city they were skirting, or that Freya's objective was elsewhere.

The sun hung low in the western sky by the time Freya turned off Interstate 15, to Wise River along Route 43, otherwise known as Big Hole Road.

The blue, plum, and indigo of twilight tinged with fiery pink at the horizon heralded the rapidly approaching night, and gave the dark Big Hole River, flowing parallel to the road, an ominous feel.

Freya paid no attention to their surroundings.

She knew exactly where she was. She had traversed this stretch of road more times than she cared to remember.

As the flicker of an occasional house danced by, Freya

counted the mailboxes until she found the one, she wanted... and dreaded.

Turning into the gloomy gravel road, she marveled how, despite running a restaurant in town, he never neglected the farm and maintained it meticulously.

She loved his dependability.

The car rumbled along the drive for several minutes, until the trees opened out and, as they followed the wide curve, the lights of the Cougar illuminated the rambling frontage of his house. A house which, he had taken pains to inform her, had been in his family since sometime in the eighteen hundreds.

Every time he told her this fact, she felt positively ante-diluvian, unable to explain, if he multiplied their length of residency by ten thousand, she would still be older.

She killed the engine and, with her gaze fixed on the porch, announced, "We're here."

Her seat tilted slightly when Sela angled her body to rest her elbows on the bucket seats.

Freya glanced at Anna, who was already rolling her eyes in disbelief that this crazy witch had dragged them across Canada to a shack in the middle of nowhere... as much as a week-old baby could roll her eyes.

The goddess braced herself for Sela's catty comment.

On cue. "Cute house. I hope whoever owns it has an indemnity policy against an onslaught from Valhalla. Do they sell Fire and Brimstone Insurance in Montana?"

"Do you have any better ideas? Do not dare say New York, we both know it's crawling with everything Odin can dredge up from the realms.

"Oh, I know, why don't we pop back to your mother-in-law's dimension? I'm sure Momma Laufey will be happy to take... wait, that's right, you tried it and I had to bring you back from the brink of..."

Their caustic repartee was cut short by the clatter of a screen door being banged against a wall.

Three pairs of eyes swiveled to a figure silhouetted in the doorway, holding what appeared to be a rifle.

"Freda Odinson, keep your butt in that car and get the hell off my property," his bellow echoed in the still air.

The distinct click of a cartridge chambering into the barrel of the Winchester 30/30 brought a pat on Freya's shoulder from Sela.

Settling back to watch the fireworks, she taunted, *sotto voce*, "*Freda*... hmmm... looks like the welcoming committee isn't in a welcoming mood."

Freya grimaced at Sela's snarky tone. Shutting her ears to her friend, she wound down her window.

"Jacob Deerstin, either drop your rifle or shove it up your ass. We both know you couldn't hit the broad side of a barn, even if the barn fell on top of you."

In truth, Jacob had earned an Expert Marksman Award while in the Army and could fire a bullet through her skull, blindfolded. It would not kill her, but it would certainly put a crimp in her evening.

"After you abandoned me, left me looking like an idiot in front of **your** wedding guests, you have the audacity to show your face on my doorstep. Give me one good reason why I shouldn't pull the trigger."

Sela and Anna squawked in surprise at this nugget of information. Their eyes swung from the man with the rifle to Freya.

Freya caught Sela in the rearview mirror mouthing the word, "*Wedding?*"

It occurred to the weary goddess how happy she would

be once she had divested herself of these two. Ignoring *that* delightful thought, she continued to plead her case.

"Because I'm not alone... and there is nobody else I dare trust."

Not only did Freya's honesty shock the other two in the car, but also it appeared to have the desired effect on the irate rancher who lowered his rifle — marginally.

"Why should I care? Hold on, let me guess, you runnin' from the law, again?"

Jacob's tone indicated this was not the first time, he had asked *Freda* that question.

Sela made a mental note to extract *that* story.

"If it helps get us in the house, Jacob, yes. You couldn't turn a newborn out into the cold night. I know it's not in you."

"Yours?" Jacob accused.

"No. She is the daughter of my friend in the backseat, and they could use a bath and a good night's sleep..." adding with a winning smile, "...and we could all use some of your cooking."

At first, the man on the porch was unmoved by Freya's entreaty.

None of this was his problem.

Besides, the anger burning inside him had not abated since the day she disappeared, and it was not ready to be doused.

Rubbing his free hand against the stubble on his chin, he pondered his next move, slowly dipping the barrel of the weapon until it was pointing at the ground.

With a grudging sigh, Jacob propped the rifle against the wall of the house.

Leaning on the porch rail, he consented, "Fine, you all can spend the night... and that's it. Come morning you're on your way, and I never hear from you again. Understand?"

Freya didn't give him any opportunity to change his mind.

Alighting, she pulled the seat forwards for Sela, then rounded the car, to hoist out Anna, complete with baby seat.

All the while, Jacob's eyes were fixed on Freya's lissom figure.

Dang, he mused, *still a thing of beauty.*

He stepped aside to let the travel-worn women enter his house. Freya slipped past him, eyeing his rifle, then glanced at the fireplace noting its missing trophy.

Shaking her head, she chided, "You jackass, how did you intend to shoot me with that piece of crap. We both know it doesn't have a firing pin."

Jacob followed them in grousing, "Yeah, and now I'm gonna have to break it down to remove the cartridge."

His frown became a wicked grin.

"Tell ya what, Freda, why don't you stick around long enough for me to fix it."

'Freda' did not deign to dignify that with a response.

She walked into the kitchen; its warmth and the familiar scents, stirring memories of Sunday breakfasts in bed, savoring the home-cured bacon and Jacob's sinful seduction.

Of being naked on the couch in front of the fire, gorging on the delightful treats Jacob had whipped up...

...and of her man...

It dawned on Freya that she had spent more time in this house naked than dressed. Never mind how much weight she had put on because of Jacob's cooking.

All that... *exercise* ought to have balanced it out... apparently not.

Setting Anna's car seat on the table, she moved to the cupboards, a smile tugging at her lips when she opened the one where he kept the coffee percolator.

As expected, the cupboard was a shambles and she had to dig about to find it. The man may be conscientious where his ranch and his food were concerned but, he was a disaster when it came to tidying up.

Some things never change. Freya chuckled inwardly.

Digging through the mess of coffee mugs and discarded cookware, she found the pot wedged in the corner.

Many were the nights after sex, when they had sat at this table, naked, drinking and talking. She instructed herself to stop taking trips down memory lane and get the damn coffee on the stove.

The pot filled with water and the basket with freshly ground, gourmet coffee, Freya fired up the gleaming, commercial grade stove he had insisted on installing.

She smiled. *Once he made his mind up, the man certainly knew how to spend a dollar.*

While the coffee bubbled, she changed Anna on the barn-wood table, half an ear on Sela and Jacob's conversation as the pair approached the kitchen.

"It's Jack, Sela. The only people who call me Jacob are the bank and the people bringing me bad news, which are usually one and the same."

Freya did not bother to look up when they entered laughing, nor when Jacob admonished her for using his table, "Damn it, Freda, do ya have to do that there? Ya know my great grandfather built..."

"Yeah, yeah. When there was six feet of snow outside,

while he was battlin' a bear, during a raid by the white ranchers surrounding his land... blah, blah, blah.

"Do you think he'd have been happier knowing we had sex on it?"

Sela sank onto one of the high-backed kitchen chairs to watch their exchange, entertained by their banter, acknowledging how the two might have been a couple.

What she failed to understand was why Freya threw it all away.

Once Freya had finished the detestable diaper changing, Sela relieved the goddess of her child.

Out of courtesy for Jacob allowing them in his house, and in an inexplicable desire for modesty, she draped a towel over her shoulder, effectively covering herself and Anna, before feeding her.

Jacob sat across from Sela, waiting for the coffee. He enjoyed watching Freda bustle around the kitchen, gathering the coffee mugs and plates.

"There's some cold meat in the fridge and tea cakes in the breadbin." He waved his hand in the general direction of both storage receptacles, but figured she had not forgotten.

Freya could out-waitress the best of them at the Diner, and was best left to her own devices.

He looked at the younger woman thoughtfully.

"Might I inquire as to the whereabouts of the baby's father?" he asked tactfully.

"Gone," Sela answered with a frown. She did not want to cry in front of him so dropped her gaze to Anna.

"Sorry to hear that," Jacob replied in a fatherly tone. "Seems to happen quite frequently around here."

He glanced at Freya, who was arranging crockery and a plate of cakes on the table. She pulled a truly grotesque face and stuck out her tongue, then turned to open the fridge.

Spreading plates bearing the cold cuts and slices of bread, she poured hot fresh coffee into each mug then joined them, taking a chair at Sela's side of the table.

The conversation remained awkwardly pleasant while the women assuaged their appetites and consumed half the pot of coffee.

Jacob sipped his drink, as they told tales of the road. He interjected an occasional comment, but mostly just listened.

As the chatter dwindled, he looked into the bottom of his mug, swirling what little remained, and asked casually, "So Freda, why *are* you two... three... on the run?"

Even Anna stopped feeding at the question.

All eyes turned to Freya, waiting to see what she was going to come up with.

"It's not the law, Jack. At least not this time," Freya gave him a knowing glance over her mug.

"The child's grandfather wants to take Anna away. Feels his power and influence makes him the better choice for raising her and warrants custody of the child. He blames Sela for his son's..."

Freya bit her lip, searching for a better word in an attempt not to cause Sela, who was barely holding it together, any more distress.

"Let's just say absence, and leave it at that," she concluded.

If anybody could bring trouble to his door, Jacob knew it was Freda. He supped a mouthful of coffee as he digested the story.

"How are you related to Freda?" he addressed this harmless, yet appropriate query to Sela.

Busy burping Anna, Sela was not concentrating properly, and without thinking replied, "No, Freya and I..."

"***Freya***?" Jacob's interjection stopped her mid-sentence. "*Who* the hell is Freya?"

Jacob gaped at the woman he once — still did if he was honest — considered to be the love of his life.

He believed he knew everything about her, but this threw him. *Was anything she had told him true?*

Freya, on the other hand, glared daggers at Sela, who was wincing at her mistake.

"Sela, why don't you take Anna to the guest room? You'll find it down the hall, at the back of the house. Sheets and blankets are on the top shelf of the closet."

Sela heard the implacable tone in her friend's voice. It was not a suggestion, but a direct command.

Gathering up Anna's stuff, and her half-drunk coffee, she excused herself. "Good idea. Anna needs her sleep. Thank you, Jack, for your hospitality."

Her gratitude was met with a gruff, "My pleasure," as she fled the kitchen.

Before she had cleared the archway, the heated words began to fly.

For the next few hours, a range of expletives worthy of a dockhand, with a side order of shattering crockery, bounced off the walls.

Around two in the morning, the din changed its resonance.

The front door banged shut, as the argument spilled outside. It remained static for a few minutes before the crunch of the front screen splintering, proclaimed someone had stormed back into the living room.

The unmistakable growl of the Cougar followed in short measure.

Sela heard the tires digging into the gravel and spraying rock into the night, as the car tore down the driveway.

The discordant clunk of the screen, relinquishing the last of its structural integrity, echoed through the house, and Sela heard Jacob yell...

"God damn you, Freda... Freya. Shit..."

An old truck sputtered into life and, presumably, chased the Cougar into the night.

The sudden silence was equally deafening.

The lack of noise worried Sela more than anything else.

With the Cougar gone, so was the concealment spell. Any valkyrie who happened to be nosing about would identify Anna's power with ease.

Desperately, Sela tried to wake her daughter but Anna, tucked into a nest of pillows and comforters, slept like the dead.

"Damn your genetics, Loki," Sela reproached her late husband.

She dashed into the living room, seeking anything with which to protect Anna and her from attack — her blades tucked neatly in the trunk of the Cougar.

Spotting Jacob's gun safe, she took a moment to study the locking mechanism. A quick search of Anna's nappy bag provided makeshift picks. The lock was no match for her nimble fingers, and she murmured her thanks to Loki for helping her refine *that* trick.

Rummaging through his impressive armory, most of which she wanted to steal, she found one particular weapon which would come in useful if the need arose.

Her fingers curled around the barrel of the Winchester M97 trench gun as she noted with a thrill of excitement that the barrel had been shortened, making it a true military grade shotgun.

If she ever had the chance to talk to Jacob about his collection, she was going to make sure to have him explain how he ended up with this beauty.

Sela snagged a couple of boxes of 12-gauge double-zero buckshot.

If any of the valkyrie *did* pay a visit, they would leave with holes blown through their freaking wings... and any other part of them that bled.

She secured the safe. The last thing she needed was to give any unexpected visitors unnecessary ideas *or* access to these weapons.

Retracing her steps to the guest room, Sela entered, then closed and locked the door, relieved to see her daughter had not stirred.

Sela loaded the six shells into the magazine, and chambered the first round. Moving to the center of the bedroom, she placed the shotgun on the floor next to her.

Closing her eyes, Sela withdrew her coin from her pocket, and held it over her head. She had never channeled magic this way before, but now was not the time to quibble over whether it would work.

Summoning up every bit of runic magic she could remember, Sela pleaded in a hushed tone for the concealment spell to protect all in the room.

She felt the familiar fires lap at her fingers from the ancient metal, bathing the room in a bluish hue. The intensity of the flames became too much for Sela and the coin spiraled out of her hands, erratically.

It didn't fall to the floor, but spun above her. Sela glanced at Anna, convinced the infant was responsible, but the child was curled up, baby-snores marking her slumber.

Sela grabbed the shotgun and made herself comfortable

on the floor beside the bed, facing the door, letting the coin do its own thing.

Knees bent, she balanced the shotgun between her legs and sat at the ready.

Her gaze flicked between the door and the levitating coin. The latter seemed to know what it was doing, and Sela wasn't about to question it.

EIGHT

Dawn wrapped its chilly fingers around Wise River. The streaks over the rising sun etched the markings of a possible storm, if one were to believe the old sailor's forecasts about red sky in the morning.

The frosty dew on the ground affirmed the temperature hovered around freezing. It matched the figurative chill inside the homestead, blanketed in the uncomfortable stillness which had descended following the blowout between Freya and Jacob.

Sela's legs were stiff and numb.

She wobbled as she heaved herself upright, pins and needles from the blood surging into her legs not helping her mood.

Steadying herself on the edge of the bed, she bent to pick up her coin from the carpet.

Evidently sometime during the night, both her strength and magic had run out, and she had dozed off.

She cursed her weakness at letting it happen. Some

warrior this age had turned her into. In the old days she could have...

Taken on the entire herd of Norse gods with one hand tied behind your back. Anna giggled slyly in Sela's brain.

She glowered at her daughter, who was stretching her chubby limbs.

"How many times do I have to tell you..." Sela started but did not bother to finish, faced with an innocent, cherubic smile.

"For such a beautiful child, you do know how to wind people up don't you? Wherever your father is, he must be immensely gratified by how much you take after him."

"Yeah, but you love me anyway."

With the blood circulating properly, Sela lifted her daughter from the bed and cracked the door open cautiously.

Peering around the frame, she peered along the hallway for any signs of movement.

"Did you hear whether either of them came back last night?" she asked Anna, who was trying to nestle closer to her mother for warmth.

"I will never understand why you all prize these bodies so much. You're either cold, hungry, or poopy... and right now, I'm all three," the child protested. "And no, the house has been quiet as a grave since you fell asleep."

Making sure the shotgun was tucked under her other arm, Sela padded to the kitchen.

At the archway, she stopped to survey the room. Broken crockery was strewn everywhere.

Anna chuckled. "Think anybody survived?"

Sela picked her way through the mess, stubbing her toe on a dented pan. Traces of blood speckled the stainless steel surface.

"Highly unlikely."

Finding the coffee pot miraculously untouched on the stove, she scavenged through the opened cupboards for something to pour it in. She settled for a bowl.

Desperate times and all.

Filling it just below the rim, she was surprised to find it somewhat warm and tasty.

Righting one of the chairs with her foot, she made herself comfortable.

Rocking Anna, Sela could not help but kiss the infant, cooing softly, "You might be older than me in your mind, but these moments, forging an invisible bond, are precious and to be cherished. I'll be sad when you no longer need me for sustenance."

"With the way my father ate... are you sure?" Anna's reply made Sela wonder how much her daughter knew about Loki.

Sela presumed the girl... or whatever her true persona was... could draw the memories from her mind, but she remained curious about the connection the two might have had prior to Anna being brought into this world.

Shrugging, Sela let the child feed.

"You know she left us here, don't you."

Anna was more intent on breakfast than responding to questions, but Sela continued talking. It filled the void.

She had grown to hate the dead silence in the pit and this was equally unnerving.

"We're gonna have to figure out where to go from here." She paused to gulp another mouthful of coffee, lamenting when she realized, "Grrr... she still has my blades, too. I hope Jack wasn't too attached to his trench gun, because it looks like it will be coming with us."

Sela did not relish the thought of hitchhiking through Montana with a baby in tow, though Freya had not left them with much choice.

With the money gone and New York almost twenty-five hundred miles away, it was going to be a long walk.

While her daughter staunched her voracious appetite, Sela foraged through the refrigerator and cupboards for anything she could take with them.

If Jacob had caught up with the fleeing goddess, she probably took his head... and whatever other body parts she deemed deserving of detachment... with her.

Which means, this isn't so much stealing, as it is making sure things didn't go to waste, Sela justified.

It did not take long to accumulate a small pile of dry cereal and fruit. Sela struck paydirt when she discovered Jacob's horde of jerky.

She cleaned him out of his packets of deer and elk. More out of curiosity about their taste than actually needing them, she purloined a few packs of his bear and bison, as well.

Satisfied she was adequately stocked, Sela padded to the main room and settled Anna on the rug next to the fireplace.

Her face scrunched as she set her daughter on the thick mat with a, "Just don't think about what they got up to here."

She began to search the house in earnest for other supplies they would require.

A trickle of excitement ran through her when she stumbled across Jake's hiking gear. She tested a couple of the backpacks for weight, before finding a smaller one which sat comfortably on her back and shoulders.

Conveniently, a sleeping bag was already attached to it.

Sela also found a pair of women's hiking boots which had been tossed in the corner. It did not take her long to realize this was Freya's gear.

It saddened Sela to think that even though Jacob must have been devastated when Freya left, he could not bring himself to throw away her stuff.

Banishing that thought, Sela ransacked the rest of Jacob's closets.

Appropriating a couple of his flannel shirts and a stack of T's, she rolled them neatly into the pack, along with extra socks.

Taking the pack, she returned to the kitchen to collect the food. Adding as many bottles of water as would fit, she was as set as she could be.

Sela tugged on one of the shirts. The warm flannel had a man's scent about it, prompting her to hope Freya had given Jacob one last tumble before she killed him.

She bundled Anna into another shirt.

Hoisting the backpack over one shoulder and slinging the shotgun over the other, Sela surveyed the rooms one last time for anything useful.

Spying Jacob's hunting knife in its sheath, she swiped both, gathered up Anna, and started for the door.

The rumble of an old truck approaching along the gravel driveway arrested her flight. Unwilling to take any chances, she locked the front door, and hurried through the house to the back.

The burnished doorknob rattled insistently, accompanied by a familiar voice complaining, "Dammit, Jack, can't you do anything right?"

"Whatcha bitchin' about now, Freya," a tired, and extremely frustrated voice answered.

"Did you or did you not lock this bloody door last..."

Sela opened the door, in full escape regalia.

The pair gaped, stunned at her appearance.

"I did," she confessed.

"I see you helped yourself to my house while you were at it. Did you at least leave me anything for breakfast," Jacob sniped as he stomped indoors, relieving her of his trench gun as he passed.

"I have jerky," Sela offered meekly.

Gone were the days of mirth and merriment within the halls of Valhalla.

What remained was Odin's berserker rage at the loss of his prized spear, Gungnir, and the disappearance of the hybrid spawn of that reprobate Loki and his venomous jezebel.

Fearing Odin's retribution for even the slightest perceived breach of one of his insane edicts, the gods who risked sharing his table, were few and far between.

Unhinged and dangerous, the Asgardian had driven all but the most rabid of the deities into hiding.

None bore the brunt of his fury more than the valkyries.

Odin pinned the blame for losing the child squarely on them. He accused the valkyries of plotting against him in retribution for the judgment meted out to their treacherous twins, Herja and Svipul.

His uncontrolled wrath had caused him to strike down their healer, Eir, for attending to one of her sisters whom he had beaten to the very edge of death. The girl's crime — daring to explain why they had been unable to locate Sela or the child.

Odin demanded Eir's body be left where it fell as a warning to all that failure was longer tolerated.

It also served as a rotting reminder to Odin of Freya's fate for her betrayal.

A single night at Jacob's extended to many, in the main, because Freya had wrapped her prized Cougar around a tree in her mad dash from the homestead.

Freya and Jacob had hashed out most of their past over pastries at his diner while waiting for the tow truck to show up.

Even after the car was repaired, the three squatters seemed in no haste to leave.

Losing track of how long they had been under his feet, Jacob consented to them staying, indefinitely. The trio accepted his offer gratefully, and soon settled into a routine on the farm.

To ensure their safety from the prying eyes of the valkyries and Odin, the trio attempt to conceal the ranch all the way to its borders.

The amount of energy required to achieve this would be the equivalent of sending up a ship load of signal flares, so they needed to be quick with the spell.

Placing Anna in the middle of the property to provide an axis for the magic, Sela and Freya walked the four directions of Jacob's land.

Watching them chant their ridiculous tune to the sky, he teased, "Neither of you will scrounge up a drop of rain unless you put more shake in your tails. My people figured that out centuries ago."

To which Sela and Freya flipped him off in unison, without missing a beat.

Once the land was hidden from the Norse, they repeated the procedure at Jacob's Diner in town.

Sela and Freya agreed to work as waitresses there in exchange for rent. The agreement did not bother Sela in the least, and meant she got to wear jeans and her boots to work, eventually adding a ball cap to her outfit.

Plus, it gave her ready access to sharp cutlery if a situation necessitating it ever arose.

She considered it a double win.

Freya had not lied, Jacob's steaks were the best she had ever tasted.

Despite Freya's unceremonious flight from Wise River, scant weeks ago... leaving her fiancé holding the bouquet, so to speak... Jacob's hurried explanation about a family emergency and that she would doubtless be back in due course, had appeased those who knew and liked Freya.

That she reappeared so quickly, merely confirmed Jacob's assertion.

A few of the locals tried to wheedle the, presumably, gory details — for what else could cause a woman so obviously in love to vanish — out of Freya, who satisfied them with a, "Oh, you know how toxic some families can be? Well, mine wrote the book. One minute it's the end of the world, the next it's forgotten. I'm hopeful there will not be a repeat. It was rather harrowing."

Her statement, accompanied by a suitably anguished expression, struck a chord with the majority. They found themselves respecting her discretion and left her alone.

There was one, however who was not so forgiving. Jacob's brother, Randy. It had been his onerous task to inform Jacob, Freya had vanished into thin air, with no note or hint of her reason.

He had been the one to watch his brother's face leach of all colour, and age in front of his eyes, as he crumpled onto a pew in disbelief. The one who dragged Jacob to bed every night for two weeks after he had tried to drink away his devastation. In fact, Randy swore he had actually heard his brother's heart splinter into a million pieces.

When he heard Freya was back, he confronted her at the Diner.

"How dare you?" he roared, bursting through the door like a tornado. "You selfish bitch. After everything Jacob did for you, after the way you treated him, you have the effrontery to crawl back here? You deserve to rot in Hell."

Freya, who had dreaded this moment, closed her eyes... *if only you knew*, she thought.

Jacob came out from behind the counter to intervene, but Freya shook her head.

"It's okay, Jacob, Randy's right," she said with a sad smile. "I behaved abominably—"

"At least you got that right," Randy sneered, contempt oozing from him. "Did you bother to check whether he was okay? Did you? No... it was like you had died, worse, in fact. At least if you had died, he could grieve at your grave. Bit hard when there's no body." His lip curled in disgust.

He jabbed a finger at her. "You don't belong here. Pack your bags and piss off."

Blasted by Randy's... not unpredictable... tirade, Freya actually took a couple of steps back. His features were so contorted with fury, she feared he might actually resort to violence.

Her chest pinched. His was a righteous anger and, although her reasons for fleeing were laudable, Jacob's safety being her sole priority, she could not deny that her timing had been execrable.

Randy turned his ire on his brother. "And you, Jacob, are you stupid? Have you forgotten what she did to you? Stop thinking with your dick for one freaking second."

Regardless of what had happened... and the whole town knew anyway... Jacob, was not prepared to let Randy air their dirty laundry in public.

"Get out." he said implacably. "I get you are upset, and thank you for standing up for me, but I'm a big boy, and this is between Freya and me."

Randy squared up to his brother and started to speak, but Jacob raised his palm. "I said enough. Until you are prepared to sit down and discuss this like an adult, it's best you leave."

"The pair of you deserve each other, Tactless and Reckless." He waved his hand and stormed out, slamming the door behind him.

"Jacob..." Freya pressed a slender hand on his arm. The last thing she wanted to do was to cause a rift between the brothers. *Would she ever be able to make this right...?*

"Not here, Freya," Jacob's tone brooked no argument, and he went back to what he had been doing.

It was a long time before the siblings spoke again.

Interestingly, Jacob proved to be the more intransigent of the pair. Randy reached out occasionally, but Jacob ignored him.

"He's not a child anymore," he had said to Freya when she begged him to meet Randy half-way. "Okay, so I was a mess, but it's done. He needs to get over himself."

"Be fair, Jacob. He was only looking out for you. You should be glad of a brother who has your back. Trust me, they are a dying breed. Please don't argue over me. I am not worth it "

"That's as maybe, but you don't get to tell me what your worth is, or how I deal with my brother. You forfeited that right when you walked out, and he didn't need to be yelling at me in my own Diner. No excuse for that."

Unwilling to be responsible for another ruined relationship, Freya was not about to sit back and wait for Jacob to come around. She seized every opportunity and employed her considerable talents to reunite the brothers, but it was several months before Jacob began to thaw.

The seasons changed, and the days fell into a comfortable pattern — tranquil, untroubled, and safe.

For the next few years, this was their life.

Sela, especially, came to appreciate the wide-open spaces, the endless blue skies, and the silence of the crystal clear nights.

To stare at the innumerable stars glittering in the vast darkness — so close, Sela was certain she could reach out and pluck them like apples from a tree — gave her a sense of peace.

Sela observed Freya renounce her vanity to welcome the hint of a tan, farm life in Montana painted on her skin. She wore the fine lines which developed gracefully at the edges of her eyes like a badge of honor, unaware they emphasized the shimmering blue of her gaze.

The two women also helped out around the farm... or rather it was Sela who shouldered most of the chores because as Freya insisted, airily, peasant work was demeaning and gave her calluses.

The pair *did* impress Jacob with their ability to break and handle the horses.

Jacob had not forgotten Freya's skill when she had first appeared in his life but was surprised at the ease with which the younger woman tamed even the wildest of stallions. Obviously he had no knowledge of her background, and had assumed Sela was a poor city girl, way out of her league.

Wiser than either woman gave him credit for, Jacob knew better than to compliment them.

To Sela and Anna, Jacob's counsel was akin to that of a caring father, one with a wealth of life experience and prepared to step up when necessary.

Gradually, his placid yet solid presence helped Sela

accept Loki's... absence. She still could not bring herself to say death.

Not an easy feat when his bewitching eyes glimmered at her every time she met Anna's gaze.

As for the relationship between mother and daughter, Sela doted on Anna, only laying down the law with her when necessary.

Eventually, Freya — by dint of dogged determination — managed to persuade Jacob to reconcile with Randy.

Despite the usual arguments between siblings, they had always been close. The past few months were the longest they had gone without speaking and, for a time, their rift seemed too wide ever to breach.

It took some uncharacteristic grovelling on Freya's part, but she managed to broker a tentative truce. Slowly, contact between the brothers extended from terse text messages to actual telephone conversations, to a face-to-face meeting.

There might have been a few choice words bandied about, and quite possibly a less than polite ultimatum... should Freya ever consider a repeat performance... but the day Jacob and Randy bumped shoulders over a couple of bottles of Pabst was the day Freya finally relaxed.

Anna reveled in their Montana days, using the time to grow stronger in body and in magic.

During her first year, she learned to control the concealment shield without the aid of Freya or her mother, and no longer needed to draw her magical strength at Sela's expense.

Her shield provided better protection for her quickly developing talents.

By the time she was two, Anna had mastered the art of transdimensional teleportation. A trick which resulted in a mother's hysterical phone call to the Sheriff's department about kidnapped children when Sela discovered her missing.

Anna, it transpired, had decided to pay her grandmother a visit to demonstrate her new skill.

Grandma Laufey had swatted the child on her butt, reprimanded her for doing so without permission, and dispatched her back to her own realm immediately.

While ecstatic at Anna's developing abilities, Laufey was saddened Loki would never meet his beautiful daughter.

Meanwhile, Sela, Freya, and Jacob had torn the house apart looking for Anna.

They discovered the girl back on her bed, happily munching baked goodies from a mysterious bag, while trying to scrub a kiss off her cheek. She handed her mother a note in ancient Norse which asked Sela to let her daughter visit Grandma Laufey, more often.

Jacob had long since learned not to ask questions about what was happening on his farm.

When the Sheriff arrived, intent on commencing a statewide search for the child, Jacob explained, sheepishly, that he had taken the toddler into town for a treat without thinking to apprise her mom.

Fortunately for all, Jacob's assurance it would never happen again, accompanied by some of his famous cookies, satisfied the officer and averted the threat of a call to Family Services, which nobody wanted.

At four years old, Anna could talk the hind legs of a donkey, holding conversations with an ease more suited to a child twice her age.

Her love of reading, and ability to soak up information like a sponge attested to her astounding intellect. That along the way, she had amassed an impressive range of profanities which both amused and horrified her mother was neither here nor there.

When Anna reached the age of six, she began hand-to-hand combat training with her mother.

Sela took great pride in seeing her daughter's natural dexterity in wielding the four-foot, wooden martial art's staff she had carved for Anna, and the bowie knife Jacob had presented to the little girl.

"Doesn't every kid need a 6-inch blade?" Jacob claimed when Sela found it under Anna's pillow.

Sela did not object to her daughter's new possession... she was a swordswoman herself. What upset her was that Jacob had beaten her to giving Anna her first blade.

Mindful of Anna's tender years and taking care not to inflict serious injury on the child, Sela was, nevertheless, a hard taskmistress. She instilled in Anna the knowledge that, should a weapon be drawn in a confrontation, only one person would be left standing.

Sela wanted to ensure it would always be Anna.

The little girl even sported a small scar on her chin,

similar to her mother's, earned when she lost focus during a training session.

Homeschooling meant Ann did not have to explain to the authorities that she was caught off guard, and her mother had jabbed her in the chin with the staff.

It was a lesson Anna never forgot. Listening to her mother's teasing laughter was deterrent enough.

Grizzled Jacob may have been on the outside, but he was putty when it came to Anna who had him wrapped around her little finger.

He loved the little girl as though she was his own granddaughter and, with no children of his own, gladly took Anna under his wing to instruct her in the art of survival.

Once Jacob deemed Anna an appropriate age, he trained her to hunt and track with the best of them. Taught her how to skin and field-dress game. Age-old techniques Jacob had learned from his father, knowledge passed down through hundreds of generations of the Crow tribe.

To educate someone in the ways of his people, warmed him.

Of all the skills in which he coached her, Jacob gained the greatest pleasure in teaching Anna how to shoot, and Anna took to it with the same zeal as the old man.

When Anna was strong enough to demonstrate to Jacob that she could hold her staff steadily in one outstretched hand, he presented her with a .22 caliber *Remington* rifle which had sat neglected in his collection.

He had teased the child about having to start her out on a popgun because he wasn't sure she could handle a real gun.

Anna was determined to prove him wrong. She looked forward to the day she could make him eat his words and attain free access to his collection.

Until then, she took great care in oiling and cleaning her rifle.

The pair spent hours in the fields for target practice. When they grew bored with killing paper targets, they moved on to a shooting competition.

Something Sela would have objected to, vehemently, had she found out.

The trick shots the two attempted, occasionally bordered on the extremely dangerous. Jacob made sure Anna did not cross that line, but neither did he stifle the child's aptitude.

A former serviceman, Jacob's aim — should Anna *ever* elect to join the military — was to ensure every army in the world would want to recruit her.

That said, there was only one branch of the US service, he would permit her to join, and informed her of this every chance he got.

Anna's response was to tilt her head to one side, twirl a lock of her hair around one finger, and nod.

Periodically, she came close to beating his score, but his ego refused to let her win, adding to the entertainment value.

TEN

L ife ticked along undisturbed for the most part. Pending invasions and bloody wars with the valkyries took a backseat, supplanted by other, more worldly, concerns — the most serious being a global pandemic.

Grateful to be living in the middle of nowhere, the slightly eccentric family ensured they followed all the guidelines, endlessly glad they were able to keep the Diner open to serve their community — albeit sometimes limited to takeaway only — during what everyone agreed was a most challenging period.

Mid-November, the year Anna turned eight, Jacob broached the idea of a turkey hunt to Pine Ridge. Anna was thrilled; her first turkey hunt... she was definitely on board.

Sela's misgivings were quashed when Jacob reassured her Anna was ready for the trip.

Furthermore, the pair guaranteed they would return with enough Merriam's turkeys to stock the chest freezer for winter... or at least until they were sick of turkey meat.

After waving off the intrepid duo in their heavily laden Chevy pickup, Sela assumed management of the diner.

She had worked there long enough that the townsfolk viewed the pretty, single mother as a permanent fixture. She was always quick to fill a cup or, beaming with pride, share a picture of her daughter.

The ranch wives kept trying to fix up Sela with their eligible sons or nephews, while the ranchers joked about taking her away from this greasy diner to give her a life of luxury.

She smiled and declined the offers politely, or reminded the men they already had wives waiting at home who would probably be happy if their husbands remembered to put the seat down when they were done.

There was no one else she could love, and thinking about Loki hurt her heart; so, she buried his memory deep, deep down, painted a smile on her face, and immersed herself in work.

Darkness fell earlier at this time of year and Sela closed the diner accordingly. Customers did not want to brave the night or the threat of snow for a hot drink and a Danish.

On this particular day, Sela had sent the other waitresses home early to enjoy the evening with their families. Freya was with her, which meant the duo did not need the extra help — or payroll expense.

Freya dropped a couple of bucks in the jukebox. The soft neon gave the dimly lit diner a warm ambience. Choosing a couple of old Patsy Cline songs, she swayed to the beat.

Sela leaned against the counter enjoying the music, uninterrupted by the hub of chatter or the clink of plates. Watching Freya, Sela was revisited by the urge to ask what had happened the day her friend was supposed to marry Jacob. It would entertain her while she cleaned, a task Freya was avoiding — as usual.

"What's the story?" The question was out before Sela could stop it.

"Excuse me?" Her eyes closed, Freya danced with her invisible partner.

"Jack, I mean he's a sweetheart of a guy and all, once you get past all that stubble, but he doesn't strike me as typical of *your* consorts."

Freya shrugged, gliding across the floor in the silence between the songs. "He's always been the knight in shining armor. It's impossible for him to ignore a damsel in distress."

Sela wanted more details, and this definitely sounded like it had the makings for an interesting tale. She busied herself wiping down the counters, hoping to keep Freya talking.

"Come on, Freya. There's got to be more to it than that? I mean he's cute, in... in a Jack sort of way but, he's not..." Sela searched for the right word to describe who she considered to be Freya's ideal man. Only one came to mind, and she hated saying it, "...he's not Loki."

Patsy Cline began crooning *Crazy* in the background, coloring Freya's story.

"Not everybody has to be him, you know. It was abundantly clear you had become more than just Loki's *project* after he found you in Niflheim." Freya was deliberately tactless, giving Sela a split-second of regret for initiating the conversation.

"To my surprise I liked you, but that didn't mean it was easy being around the pair of you being all lovey-dovey." Freya stuck finger down her throat and gagged.

"I was becoming jaded, and a change of scenery was essential to —what do you humans say? — save my sanity and recharge my batteries. I was already in this realm, so it seemed as good a place as any... and you know how that ended."

Freya, who had shared the details of her *Grand Tour* and torrid affair with a handsome Irish bartender, heard Sela chuckle. "Don't start," she admonished.

"As if." Sela assumed an innocent expression.

"Brat," Freya retorted. "I thought seeing Loki with you was hard, but discovering you carried his child, nearly killed me... and I'm immortal. My reaction was—"

"Catty? Bitchy? Shrewish? All of the above?" Sela interjected impishly, recalling Freya's outburst at her wedding.

"Insensitive," Freya countered loftily. "It came as a shock and I admit to being a trifle... irrational, so sue me."

Sela stretched across to squeeze her friend's hand. "You were not a happy chappie."

"Jealousy is an insidious emotion, hon. Anyway, I left New York and Jack found me broken down in a ditch along Highway 212 during a rainstorm. I guess he took pity on me."

Freya's inadequate explanation triggered more questions.

"What were you doing driving in Montana in the first place? Especially if the storm was that bad. You drive like shit when the sun is out. Besides you are a goddess and could have poofed yourself anywhere. Wait... was Jack serious when he asked if you were running from the cops again the night we arrived?"

Elbowing past Sela, Freya lifted a beer out of the cooler. Popping the top, she tipped the bottle at Sela, and smiled innocently. "Take it out of my paycheck."

Freya swallowed a mouthful, savoring the amber brew. "I was tired of magic. It always gets me in trouble. Saving you is a perfect example." She winked.

"As for the police, that was a misunderstanding caused by some sore losers running a Reservation Casino outside the town of Crow Agency. They had become a little suspicious of my incredible winning streak, and weren't crazy about me *borrowing* a tribal truck on my way out."

Sela shook her head in benign resignation, as she listened to Freya's story.

She had reconciled herself to Freya's almost human frailties, long since, but had yet to come to terms with the fact, the most revered goddess of the Norse pantheon was, at heart, a con artist and, evidently — a car thief.

"Are you telling me, somewhere out there is an outstanding warrant with your name on it?" Sela grinned.

"Regrettably, probably for poor Freda Odinson, at least. That is if the statute of limitations hasn't run out," Freya contemplated that question, while Sela re-evaluated her opinion regarding Freya's knowledge of the legal system.

"Anyway, instead of turning me into the law, Jack took

me back to his place. I guess aiding and abetting is one of his character flaws. Never did ask him why."

Freya sipped her beer, contemplatively.

Since her return, Jacob and she had not revisited renewing their relationship. That he had not kicked them out was enough.

It was a necessary decision at the time, she acknowledged to herself. *Now, it is just foolish not to sit down and confront him about the future... if we have one.*

"Speaking of which, why Freda," Sela needled, "...and Odinson? Couldn't you come up with a better alias?"

"Do you know my last name?" Freya replied, between gulps of beer.

"I assumed none of you deities had one, you know, like Cher." Sela giggled, nudging her.

"Been so long since I used it, I don't even think I could pronounce it," Freya said into her bottle, with a wistful smile. "It never ceases to amaze me that Midgardians believe we materialized out of thin air.

"That would be a legendary feat." She drained the drink. "As for why I used Odin's name." She shrugged. "We were supposed to be the ultimate power couple, weren't we? Maybe one day the story tellers will get it right."

Sela felt bad asking Freya the *$64,000 Question,* but the latter had gone too far for her not too.

"So why didn't you marry Jacob when you had the chance?"

Freya got up from the stool and circled the counter to throw away the empty bottle. She looked into the can, amused at how metaphorical coincidences occurred at the strangest times.

Yeah, I certainly have a way of trashing everything, Freya mused inwardly.

To Sela, she said, "He's human."

"Duh, I know that which doesn't explain anything." Sela was not letting Freya off that easily.

"Why do you think you are immortal? Because you earned it?" Freya narrowed her eyes. "Hardly. It is because Loki couldn't stand the thought of losing you... *ever*. Now *he's* gone, how does it feel to spend eternity without him?"

"In that case, why didn't you make Jack an immortal? Seems easy enough for you people to do, even if you're not asked to."

"I couldn't do that to him," Freya confessed. "To take away his humanity and force him to watch his friends and family die. Not even I am that selfish. Besides, if you haven't noticed, Jack is Native American, Crow to be exact — and yes, the irony of him saving me from his own tribal police doesn't escape me either."

No less confused about where this part of the story was going, Sela pressed, "And?"

Freya sighed before she answered, "Sela, you more than anyone should understand Odin's belief in pure blood lines. Why did you think he was so opposed to Loki claiming you?

"It is the same fanaticism held by the deities in all cultures. It is supposed to assure perpetual rule. Or so the fallacy goes."

Freya spotted a long-forgotten picture of the two of them. Jacob had hung it up on the wall behind the bar, but she had not noticed it until now.

The fading photograph had caught them looking at each other, their love a tangible thing, eliciting a sad smile as she traced the image with gentle fingers.

"Jack's life would have ended the day he said *I do*. Odin would not permit me to marry someone of a different —

hmmm, how do I put this politely? — genesis. You could be forgiven for accusing Odin of being the original racist."

Sela felt they had reached the proverbial awkward point in the conversation. "Let's call it a night and go home. 'Sides, I need you fresh in the morning to slave over breakfast."

Freya's answer was to get her coat and walk to the door, slowing when a figure, shrouded in the darkness, loomed up on the other side of the glass.

The glass door rattled insistently. Apparently, this customer was unable to comprehend the meaning of a *Closed* sign.

"Read the sign, buster, we're closed," Sela shouted at the figure, who paused.

"There'll be plenty of biscuits and gravy waiting for you when we open at five tomorrow," Freya was moved to console.

The dark shape backed up from the door, and dropped its hood. Blue flames appeared at the end of each arm, illuminating a woman who flashed the briefest of smiles at the pair through the glass.

It was none other than Sanngriðr, the craziest and most violent of Odin's personal valkyries.

Before either Sela or Freya could utter a word, the façade of the diner imploded. The intensity of the blast flung the pair over what remained of the counter.

Sanngriðr looked at her palms, awed by the power, then at her handiwork, reminding herself to thank mighty Odin for her new gifts. In her mind, she had always deserved them anyway.

Destruction was wasted in the hands of my pathetic sister, Herja.

She stepped through the rubble and scrutinized the stunned duo.

"Ladies," she trilled. "You have *no* idea how happy I am to find you!"

"Fuck you, Sanngriðr," Freya reverted to the deliciously succinct human expletive as she rose to her feet. "I shouldn't be surprised to see you, but how?"

Blood dripping from a gash at the corner of mouth, Sela was slower to rise, but joined Freya to face the valkyrie.

Pulling the dagger from her boot, Sela challenged, "So the Old Man can't handle his own fights anymore? Has to send his lackeys?"

Sanngriðr laughed at the impudence. "Imagine our surprise when we discovered a quaint little farm had sprung up in the middle of nowhere. Now *how* do you suppose that happened?"

She opened her palms, and struck again.

Chairs and tables splintered everywhere, prompting Sela and Freya to bolt in opposite directions to avoid the assault as the diner was torn apart in front of them.

The valkyrie chuckled. "I reduced that pretty little plot of land to a pile of embers. Such a shame but, given I could not find your little bitch there, what choice did I have?"

Rage consumed the two women who realized their false sense of security had left them complacent. Neither had thought to re-establish the Concealment Spell after waving goodbye to Anna and Jacob.

"Anna," Sela screamed.

Her daughter could be facing an army of valkyries at this moment.

Enjoying the devastation, she was wreaking, Sanngriðr was not paying attention to anything the women were saying.

She did pause to add, "If you two would be so kind as to hand her over, your deaths will be quick, and painless... well, maybe."

Taking advantage of the momentary lull in the valkyrie's onslaught, Freya and Sela attacked.

Freya cast pure energy at Sanngriðr trying to expel her from the diner. The valkyrie responded with a fireball, which catapulted Freya into the kitchen, wrenching the door off its hinges in the process.

Despite wanting to check on her friend, Sela did not have that luxury.

Leaping onto Sanngriðr's back, Sela hooked her arm around their attacker's throat, and hung on for dear life, jabbing her dagger into the valkyrie with ferocious repetition.

Sanngriðr howled in pain, thrashing wildly in an attempt to dislodge the vicious wildcat.

Staggering, and slamming Sela against anything she could, Sanngriðr managed to snag a handful of Sela's hair. Snarling it in her fingers, she hurled Sela into the wall.

The Midgardian's body slumped to the floor, in a motionless heap. Sanngriðr kicked Sela in the head just to make sure she stayed that way.

Satisfied she had taken care of the whore, she marched to the kitchen, blowing the remains of the doorframe from the wall with a flick of her hands.

Entering the dark room, she ignited a fireball in her palms to use as a weapon and a torch. Scanning the floor for Freya's body, she grumbled in disappointment when it was not to be seen.

Her attention shifted to the glimmer of a street light bleeding through the open backdoor.

Sprinting across the kitchen, Sanngriðr yelled to the empty street, "Run you craven coward. I'll find you again."

She felt a tap on her shoulder.

Pivoting on her heel to find out who dare touch her, she came face to face with Freya.

The Goddess of Sex had morphed into a Warrior of Hate.

Engulfed in a fiery shroud, her voice echoed with an unnatural resonance, "Craven coward huh? Kiss Hel's ass for me when you see her in Helheim, bitch."

Before Sanngriðr could react, Freya concentrated all her energy into a single bolt, zapping it into Sanngriðr's chest and kept the connection between them.

Throwing her arms outwards, she ripped the valkyrie apart.

The intensity of her enmity demolished the kitchen, and nothing remained of Sanngriðr save a few smoldering ashes on the floor.

Hearing the creak of a building on the verge of collapse, Freya picked her way through the debris in search of Sela.

Spotting her friend, bleeding and unconscious on the floor, Freya scooped her up and dashed out through the hole which was once the frontage. She did not look back as their beloved diner disintegrated.

Certain Sela was dead, Freya laid her on the sidewalk. She had never attempted to bring the same person back from the dead a second time, but she needed her now.

Tears filled Freya's eyes as she raised her hands in an attempt to summon all the magic nature harbored. She had barely begun her chant, when she was interrupted by a dry question.

"If you're done singing the song of your people, oh wondrous Goddess, might we save my daughter?"

Freya gave a startled squeak and gathered her friend into a tight hug. "I'm afraid the *No magic* rule just went up in flames... literally.

"Whatever you do, don't let go."

As the whine of the approaching fire trucks harmonized with the siren of the Sheriff's car, the pair vanished into the wind.

CHAPTER
ELEVEN

T he cold November night enveloped the well-stocked campsite.

Jacob was a firm believer that roughing it did not necessarily mean *roughing it*.

The coolers were stacked with sodas for Anna, and beer for himself.

The small tents ensured everything stayed nice and dry, while the sleeping bags, rated to minus ten degrees, guaranteed a warm night's sleep.

The rainbow trout, Jacob had caught for dinner was barbecuing over the campfire, the air redolent with the aroma of Jacob's gourmet, heartland cooking.

Once their appetite was slaked, the pair relaxed around the fire planning the next day's turkey hunt.

Anna wagered she would double anything Jacob managed to bag. He chuckled that by law she had to stop at nine. The child feigned a bratty pout at being limited to such a puny number.

The remnants of their food cleared away, Jacob noticed Anna staring into the fire. Curiosity got the better of him.

"Too late in the year to watch the ticks explode in the heat, so whatcha looking at?" Jacob joked.

"Jack, can you keep a secret?" Anna asked, watching the flames dance.

A trifle concerned, he replied, "Kinda depends on what it is, Anna."

"Mom would be furious with me if she knew," Anna continued softly, sounding genuinely concerned about Sela's reaction if she found out.

Lousy at guessing games, Jacob, as ever when Anna talked in riddles, got straight to the point.

"Knew what, Button?" He used her nickname, the one he had made up. Not because she was cute as one — although she was — but because of her propensity to go nuclear when conversations became too personal.

He had a sneaking suspicion, this conversation was about to exceed all her boundaries.

Finally, she made eye contact with her hunting companion, "I know where my dad is."

"What? How? I thought he was..." Jacob scoured his brain for a word which would not upset Anna.

"Dead?" Canting her head, she pondered, "He is...well, sort of, I guess, but we still talk."

Uncomfortable with where this was going, Jacob sought to reassure the child that what she was experiencing was perfectly natural.

"Lotsa kids talk with their parents who are in Heaven, Button. Makes 'em feel better knowing they'll always be there for them."

"Oh, Dad's definitely not in Heaven, Jack." Anna's gaze returned to the fire. "Truth is, he's not sure where he is, but tells me he's gonna come visit us, Mom and me, when he figures out how."

The conversation had just crossed into the *Too Creepy to Continue* for Jack. He decided a subject change was a good idea. He could only try.

"How do you plan on bagging anything with that measly .22?"

Acknowledging that redirecting the conversation towards guns right at this moment might *not* have been the most judicious call, Jacob surmised it was too late to backpedal. At least it wasn't a discussion about ghostly fathers.

Anna smiled to relieve the old man's doubts. "I'm a good enough hunter to bring 'em down with a rock."

He chuckled. "Haha, I don't doubt that, Button, but I have something that might be a better alternative."

Jacob disappeared into his tent to return with a ribbon wrapped gun case. Setting the package on Anna's lap, he resumed his seat.

The girl tore through the ribbon and opened the case, squealing when she saw a brand new 12-gauge Remington shotgun.

With its shortened barrel and highly polished burl oak stock, she was ecstatic to see, Jacob had designed the gun specifically for her to hunt turkeys.

The bonfire flickered in the barrel's blue steel, which reflected in Anna's wide eyes as she studied the gun.

Carefully removing the weapon from the case, she held it in her hands, testing the weight and balance. Speechless, her gaze swung back and forth between the gift and Jacob.

"I wasn't sure I should get it for you or not, cuz it's gonna kick your ass when you fire it." Jacob grinned. "And, if your Mama asks where it came from, tell her you found it in a box of Cracker Jacks."

Scrunching up her face, Anna countered in all seriousness, "Silly, mom would know I was fibbing. I hate Cracker Jacks."

This made them laugh and, after teasing each other about the evils — or not as the case may be — of caramel-coated popcorn, they spent the next little while examining the gun.

"Jack?" Anna reverted to her serious, *I want to talk about something important,* voice.

Jacob grimaced internally given their last heart to heart. Glancing at his watch, he asked, "Can it wait until tomorrow, Button? You really should get to bed if we want that early start."

"I will, but I want to know why you've never said anything about our..." Anna hesitated, trying to find the right word, settling on, "...*uniqueness?*"

Relieved the girl was too young for the dreaded coming-of-age conversation, Jacob chuckled. "That description has *got* to be the understatement of the century, Button."

"That's what I mean. You know we possess *unusual* attributes and are capable of — for want of a better word — exploits, others are not. I love that you accept it without question, but what if something happens that scares you so much you want to run away from us?"

Jacob put his arm around Anna and gave her a grandfatherly hug, reassuring, "That will never happen."

"You can't guarant—"

"I can, Anna. As far as it is within my power, I will never let anything happen to you or your mom—"

"Or Freya?"

"Yes, Button, even Freya."

There was a weighty silence, then Anna pressed in a subdued voice, "Not even if we possess magic?"

"Anna, everybody possesses some level of magic, unfortunately they have no idea how to harness it. The magic the three of you control is older than the Earth itself. I sensed it in Freya the moment I met her."

"How? I mean, and forgive me for saying this, you're human."

"No offense taken." Jacob chuckled. "Even as a lowly human, yours truly possesses a magic passed through my people since the dawn of time. The difference between the two of us, is that your magic is aimed at discord and devastation, whereas mine is directed by nature and healing.

"In my younger days, I served my tribe as a medicine man. Do you know what that is?"

Anna nodded. She had learned its meaning from Freya.

"Then you know why you'll never get rid of this old man." Jacob tousled Anna's hair. "Now to bed with you before you come up with another campfire topic I might not be able to handle.

Anna giggled and, rising to her feet, went to her tent, weapon in hand.

Knowing he could not pry the shotgun out of Anna's clutches, Jacob used his discretion and let her take it to bed with her — on the proviso she replaced it in the case before she fell asleep.

To which he received a mournful, "Yes."

With Anna tucked in, Jacob settled into his camp chair to finish his beer before following suit. Watching the fire die down to smoking embers, he leaned back listening for the usual nighttime sounds.

All he heard was an eerie silence... and the snap of a branch.

Ice trickled down his spine as the hairs went up on his

nape. Jumping to his feet, Jacob drew his .45 from its holster and peered into the darkness for movement.

"Who's out there?"

A massive spear sheared the night, narrowly missing him as he dived out of the way.

Jacob rolled onto his stomach, shooting into the darkness, hoping if he had not hit whoever was out there, he would scare them off.

Something snagged the back of his shirt, yanking him upright. The unseen adversary hoisted him higher, requiring him to balance on his toes.

Jacob struggled to see his assailant, but all he could make out were what appeared to be... *feathers? Not possible.*

A loud flap and a soft thud jerked Jacob's attention to a feminine figure landing next to the fire. Rendered mute, he gawked in astonishment as the creature shook out its wings and folded them in, revealing a long blonde braid.

In a futile attempt to dispel the image, he blinked furiously, but the scene did not change, except the creature stormed off to the edge of the camp.

'Wings' holding him, laughed, chiding her — his captor sounded female — companion's errant aim.

"A good thing Odin didn't witness that horrendous throw, Geirdriful. He would have you scrubbing the floors."

"Shut up, Thrud. He's not here, and you will do well to keep your mouth shut," the creature sniped testily as it stooped to retrieve the spear.

Jacob watched a pair of slender, but muscular, legs kneel to dig the tip out of the cold dirt.

He heard it recite something in a language he did not understand, but was reminiscent of the strange chants Sela and Freya often muttered.

Freeing the massive spike, the creature returned to the

edge of the fire, and thrust it into the embers; the cinders illuminating her beautiful, yet irate face.

Stirring quickly, she whipped the bonfire back to life. The flames lit up the camp.

"If you are finished playing with the fire, Geirdriful, please may I tear this one apart so we can get the girl and go home? I hate coming to this realm," the one called Thrud whined.

"Patience, sister dearest. Do you see her anywhere?" Geirdriful barked. "I have faith this male will give her up to save his sorry life, won't you, human?"

Geirdriful took a step closer to Jacob, the tip of her spear glowing red from the fire. Holding it inches from Jacob's face, she watched with glee as he strove to avoid the scorching heat.

His efforts elicited a malicious snigger.

"You weak Midgardians are all the same. Self-preservation is your only strength. Tell me where to find Loki's daughter and, perhaps, I shall let you live," she demanded in heavily accented English.

Jacob bellowed when Geirdriful pressed the sizzling metal to his cheek. The excruciating agony made him spasm in Thrud's grip, nearly slipping from her grasp. His last conscious thought, that he had failed to protect Anna.

Thrud yelled at her accomplice, "*I* can't kill him, but it's acceptable for you to set him on fire? How do *you* expect him to say anything if you burn his face off?"

Their argument reverberated around the campsite becoming more absurd.

Out of the darkness, a command interrupted their inanity.

"***Stop. Do not hurt him.***"

The pair squinted in the direction of the voice. A lantern

switched on, and they saw the silhouette of a girl cast against the nylon tent.

Thrud hurled a limp Jacob to one side to confront their quarry.

Drawing her sword from its sheath, she did not bother to give the girl a chance to surrender, deciding to slice through the nylon with one slash.

The blast of the shotgun blew the valkyrie ten feet from the opening.

Thrud had never known pain like it. Instinctively, her fingers sought the source to feel the warm wetness of her blood seeping from the wound.

She howled like an injured bear.

Geirdriful did not make the same mistake.

Unfurling her wings, she launched herself into the night sky, dodging the spray of buckshot as Anna charged out of the tent, gun firing.

Casting her mighty spear, Geirdriful trusted her aim was true this time, sure it would kill the diminutive witch or at least impede her long enough for Geirdriful to retrieve Thrud's bow.

As the spear left her hand, she shrieked in anguish; the tip of her wing clipped by Anna's buckshot.

Drooping, Geirdriful fought to stay in the sky. The rents in her graceful wings made it difficult to control her flight and she crashed next to Thrud's writhing body.

Snatching her sister's quiver and bow, Geirdriful fired at Anna who, while reloading her shotgun, took refuge behind a tree.

The two exchanged barrages, each hoping the other would run out of ammunition first.

Fatigued from her injury and resulting battle with Anna, Geirdriful let out a shrill whistle.

The earth shuddered as the whole of the Odin's Valkyrie Guard appeared and encircled the camp.

Emboldened by the arrival of reinforcements, Geirdriful seized what she presumed to be her advantage.

Gathering her strength, Geirdriful ascended the best as she could. With all the control of a drunken bee, she hovered unsteadily above Anna, and emptied her quiver at her.

Anna dropped her shotgun and raised her arms over her head. Palms open, the girl halted the hail of arrows mid-flight.

Clenching her hands into tight fists, Anna ground the arrows into shrapnel and hurled them back at Geirdriful.

Catching a faceful of the projectiles, the valkyrie roared her agony, her eyes bleeding as the splinters tore into them.

Flying blind and unable to defend herself, Geirdriful became easy prey for Anna.

The girl pointed at the floundering valkyrie. Snatching her from the night sky, Anna slammed her hands together, crushing Geirdriful's body as though it was nothing more sinister than the tipsy bug she had just resembled.

She watched the mangled remains drop to the ground.

Screams whipped Anna's attention to the advancing Guard. She saw one of the valkyries tumble forwards, her head separated from her shoulders.

The glint of slashing steel caught Anna's eye as the next fell. She exhaled on a grateful whoosh, recognizing her mother's blades.

Sela and Freya had materialized at the rear of the invaders, and were fighting through the warriors, hacking and exploding bodies to reach Anna.

Anna ran to join them in combat.

She was halfway across the campsite, when she skidded to a halt spying Jacob's unconscious body alongside his pickup. Dropping to her knees, she shifted him onto his back.

Jacob's rugged, yet kindly face was marred by the ugly burn from the searing tip of Geirdriful's spear. The smell of his charred flesh curled into Anna's nose, and her stomach rebelled.

Incensed, her eyes blazed vivid red and, despite the battle raging around her, the world seemed to come to a standstill.

Freya was the first to sense the distortion in the atmosphere. Perceiving the fury building in Anna, she dragged Sela to the ground.

Struggling to pin Sela beneath her, the goddess cast a shield over them.

Accidentally being stabbed by Sela was less of a concern than whether her magic was enough to protect them from what was about to be unleashed.

The Guards were knocked off balance as Anna drew breath. The shock wave which radiated from her scream vaporized everything in its wake. It tore through the ranks of the valkyries, disintegrating them before they had a chance to flee.

The surrounding countryside fared no better. Trees were uprooted and splintered. Immense granite boulders split in half and scattered like dust in the breeze.

The once idyllic campsite had been excoriated.

Silence fell over the dark, ravaged landscape... save the sounds of a sobbing child. Tears spilled down Anna's cheeks as she tried to rouse Jacob.

"Wake up, Jack. Please, we need you."

She glanced up when a hand grasped her shoulder. Her

eyes followed her mom as she knelt next to her to examine Jack.

"Is-is he dead?" Anna asked with a woebegone hiccup, fearing the answer.

Sela checked Jacob's throat for a pulse. Though faint, there was one discernible. A relieved smile curved her lips.

That was all Anna needed. She flung her arms around Sela, hugging her tightly before repeating the gesture with Jacob.

Releasing him, she eased him back on the ground, scanning the vicinity for something warm with which to cover him, settling for the shredded remnants of her tent. She handed the ragged canvas to Freya, who had taken her place alongside Sela to try to heal the burn.

Red-eyed from her bout of weeping and the lingering effects of her cataclysmic magic, Anna looked at her mother.

"This is all my fault, Mom. I forgot to protect us."

Ignoring the fact Anna was nearly as tall as she, Sela lifted her daughter into her embrace. Their eyes met and Sela shook her head.

"No, Anna. It's not your fault, sweetheart. The blame for this lies with Odin. It always has."

Safe in her mother's arms, Anna wept into Sela's shoulder. All she ever wanted to be was an eight-year-old girl.

She kissed her mom's cheek and whispered, "We need to talk."

TWELVE

W*here do deities go when they cease to exist?*

Loki toyed with that question while he tried to figure out where he was. It wasn't Midgard, and it certainly wasn't Valhalla — although the notion of being welcomed into those hallowed halls, made him chuckle.

He pictured a resentful Odin being coerced into throwing a lavish feast to welcome home the brave hero. A river of ale and mead overflowing the horns as they drank, showering the revelers in the Hall.

Maybe the two would share a maiden or twenty, like they used to... so long ago.

Ah... the good old days.

Loki's smile brightened as he wallowed in the illusion of the drunken orgy. It was just a dream and Sela could not—

Sela!

Her name pierced his heart deeper than any wound Odin could inflict.

The vision of his wife and daughter being entombed in

the Earth, triggered a devastated howl. No one could surmount such barbarity.

There was no chance they had survived.

Yet, he had been able to talk with Anna, *hadn't he?*

He was certain it was her essence. She had told him as much, and that Sela and she were waiting for him on the other side.

The other side of what?

The swirling questions were beginning to give Loki a headache.

A more feasible explanation was that his own mounting madness had willed her to be alive. Hel had implied they perished before his own end — or whatever this nothingness was.

Wait...

Hel...

Hmmm... the one daughter who could be responsible for my current situation. Punishing me for marrying Sela was definitely within the realms of her jealousy.

Loki pushed all thoughts from his mind, except one. If he had the capacity to think, he must be somewhere... *mustn't he?*

Squinting, he scrutinized his surroundings. While apparently devoid of any solid walls or foundation, he discerned a faint gleam.

Concentrating on the glimmer, Loki reached out to investigate. Pressing the nebulous periphery of his confinement, he was startled when it sagged at his touch.

Incensed, he commanded, "Hel, release me from whatever sick dream you have trapped me in. Now."

He paused, half-expecting to hear his reprobate daughter whine that he was stealing all her fun.

All he heard was his voice thundering in the distance.

Loki lost patience with this stupid game.

Concentrating all his energy on the obstacle, he pounded on it, burrowing his fists deeper and deeper into whatever enclosed him.

Gradually, light began to filter through.

His blows quickened, each impact delivered a new ray of brilliance into his *prison* until, without warning, he pitched forwards — free at last.

Temporarily dazzled, he registered he was lying on something solid. Shielding his eyes, blinking the world into focus, all he could make out were blurry shapes looming over him.

His arms were seized and he was hauled upright. Instinctively, Loki rebelled, swinging indiscriminately at the figures, landing a decent punch or two.

Whatever held him staggered, the grip loosened. Preparing to make good his advantage, he was stalled by a hand grasping his wrist.

"Enough, Father."

It was Hel.

Called it, Loki grouched inwardly.

"It is about time you dragged your misbegotten rump through the barrier," she jeered. "I was beginning to think you decided to languish there for the rest of eternity."

"Why the devil..."

"Devil? Have you been hanging around Midgard for so long you actually believe their tall tales? The only devil here, my dear, dear Papa, is you."

Loki ignored his daughter's cynicism. "...would you put me in..." he scoured his brain for a more descriptive word for whatever limbo had incarcerated him, but there wasn't one to suit, "...that?"

Hel released her father's wrist, and ascended to her

throne. Making herself comfortable on the gaudy pile of golden bones, she shrugged.

"Don't blame me." Hel chuckled. "You were the one who put yourself in a virtual timeout. I'm only here to make sure you don't damage the place."

She popped a human eyeball into her mouth.

Chewing and talking at the same time, she mumbled, "I *really* need to have instruction manuals printed out for you new arrivals. These questions become tedious fast."

Loki dipped a bow to his daughter. "Begging your pardon, your Majesty. It was rude of me to bore you."

"Shut up," Hel tsked.

Loki obliged.

"Now that I have your attention, I would like to discuss why you are here."

"Thought it was because I was dead," Loki carped.

"That's only part of it, my dearest Father, but your presence, whilst irksome, does offer me the chance to fulfill my greatest desire. A venture, mission shall we say, one, I doubt even you would oppose."

Loki cocked a brow at his daughter. "What could that possibly be?"

"Revenge," Hel said airily as she curled her legs under her and chose another eyeball.

"Against whom, may I ask?" His daughter's motives piqued Loki's curiosity.

He paced the floor as they talked, more interested in finding a way out of this asylum than in entertaining Hel's proposal.

"If you want to waste time asking," Hel sighed, "we can start with Odin. He did murder the great love of your life, didn't he, not to mention that cute little snot of a child, or had you forgotten?"

She let that sink in, watching for a reaction.

"Oh, and adding insult to injury, his personal guard caught up with Freya." Hel smirked at her father's back. She knew this was a lie, but Loki didn't. "From what I hear, she got what she deserved. Leaving your poor family to suffer. The valkyries feasted on her remains."

Loki paused mid-stride, pivoting on his heel to scowl darkly at his offspring. Contempt radiated off him.

"Why do you care about avenging their deaths, given your undisguised animosity for both of them?"

"An error of judgment for which I shall never forgive myself." Hel feigned a sorrowful frown for good measure. "It was selfish to allow my jealousy to interfere with your happiness," Hel's disclosure was so saccharine sweet it bordered on sickening.

"I'm sorry it took their deaths for you to reach this epiphany," Loki remonstrated sarcastically, resuming his laps of the room.

He could read Hel like a book, proficient in recognizing when she was lying... typically when her lips were flapping.

Though, ridding the realms of Odin is an intriguing concept.

"Tell me, my ray of sunshine," Loki wanted details, "what do you gain from Odin's demise?"

His daughter and altruism were polar opposites.

"I get to ditch this dump. Even you have to admit, eons of being exiled here because I'm *your* daughter should be ample punishment. Isn't it time I received my discharge papers?" she elaborated.

"Wait... *a start?*" Loki stopped mid-stride to narrow his gaze at her. "What else is going on in that conniving head of yours?"

Ahhh... the heart of my plan.

Hel rose and walked over to where Loki was standing,

towering over him; every inch the daughter of a giantess. Looking down at her sire gave her a sense of superiority as she provided the pertinent particulars.

"A start in that with Odin gone, you can release my brother, Jörmungandr," Hel clarified. "He grows tired of being constrained on Earth. He wants you to give the word so he can initiate the end of everything."

Loki stared at Hel, in astonishment.

"You do realize you are both out of your minds."

He stalked off, chastising himself for his failure as a parent.

"Maybe I ought to have spent more time with you, protected you, done all those things, so-called, normal families do; parks circuses, holidays..." Blithely ignoring the fact none of the latter activities would have been remotely possible.

"At the very least I should stood up to Odin instead of ignoring your misery and galivanting around the realms—"

"Stop it." Hel scowled at Loki. "It's too late to play the *What If* game."

"Your plan is not a solution. Has it dawned on you, if I liberate Jörmungandr, his destruction will bring an end to all of the realms... including your little oasis?"

Hel nodded, "Yes, Father, I am cognizant of the legend, but I know something of which the ancient scribes were unaware," she paused for dramatic effect. "My father does not belong to this dimension."

That brought Loki up short and he listened to his daughter in earnest.

Maybe she is right, Loki ruminated. *None of the realms have treated me or any of my offspring fairly. Is it time to call it a day and go home? There is nothing left for me in either Midgard or Valhalla.*

Hel watched Loki drop into one of the dusty chairs lining the wall of her throne room. She could see the gears grinding in his mind as he mulled over her words.

"So, freeing yourself will mean killing yourself, Hel?" He met her assessing gaze.

"Hardly, Father. I'm sure there's more than enough room in your dimension for your favorite daughter. Now, let us discuss releasing my brother..."

THIRTEEN

T hey could not return to Wise River.

The radio blared a non-stop commentary from the farm, which, mysteriously, lay in ruins, and the diner — similarly obliterated.

With no hard evidence to back up their report, speculation ran wild, from domestic terrorism, to aliens, to the Rapture. Whatever the cause, that Jacob and his family had perished in the explosion at the diner was — according to everyone questioned — incontrovertible.

Sela switched off the radio and studied the people crowded into the front seat of Jacob's battered old truck.

Freya's pallid features were etched with dread.

Her chatterbox of a daughter appeared to be avoiding her as much as one could in the front seat of a '64 Chevy pickup. Whatever Anna was so eager to talk about earlier had left the girl unnaturally silent... and on the verge of tears.

Their urgency to flee the scene of the ambush, left no time for Anna to unburden herself. It had to wait until they were safe or, at least, further from danger, and Sela's heart clenched at the child's forlorn expression. *She was only eight.*

Sweetheart, no matter what is going on, I am always here for you, Sela assured through her mind. Anna did not reply.

Sela squinted at Jacob, who was wedged against the passenger door. He floated in and out of consciousness, which although worrying, offered a modicum of relief because she had neither the energy nor the desire to explain any of this to him.

Feeling the truck veering towards the ditch, she deemed it sensible to pay attention to the road. It had taken the magic of all three of them to free the pickup from the tree, it ended up wedged into during Anna's outburst.

They had tried to straighten the front axle — with marginal success — and the vehicle was crabbing badly. Wrestling with the steering wheel added to Sela's joy at this unexpected journey.

Approaching a modest travel lodge along the Montana-South Dakota border, Sela and the magic abandoned the poor vehicle. Although the brakes failed to stop them — the big green dumpster Sela hit, did not.

"Welcome to Baker, Montana, folks. Population, no one cares and our last stop until we can conjure up another form of transportation," Sela announced like a cheerful tour guide.

Humanity's misconception of magic never failed to amuse Sela.

"You can't just click your fingers and produce a car out of thin air like a Vegas illusionist, it has to come from somewhere," Freya had taught her years before.

In truth, stealing was basically sleight of hand, and this place did not appear to be brimming with suitable prospects.

On top of that, the excessive manipulation of magic required to keep their current wreck together had taxed them all.

A couple of nights in a nondescript, border-town motel did not sound too arduous and, thanks to Anna's stunt, the number of valkyries who might *bump into them* had been reduced — drastically.

"Anyone have cash?"

Sela held out her hand for donations, to receive nothing more than the uncomfortable stares associated with an empty church offering plate.

"My purse was lost in the diner." Freya shrugged apologetically, "I'm pretty sure Jack's billfold went up along with half of Pine Ridge."

"Well, that sucks," Sela observed, lowering her arm.

Giving it some thought, she came up with a solution, albeit temporary.

Placing her coin in her palm, she concentrated on its composition and details. Harnessing the last of her strength, she duplicated the gold piece.

Some museum's inventory is gonna come up short, she thought before dismissing any concerns over where it might have come from.

The new coin contained none of the magical properties steeped in Sela's, yet was perfectly able to perform its own wonders.

Judging the weight of the gold in his hand, the motel owner was persuaded to overlook the dented bin, simultaneously affirming that, miracle of miracles, he *did* have adjoining rooms available.

He reckoned the coin would cover a couple of nights, might even stretch to some of his wife's cooking as a hospitality bonus.

Of course, guest confidentiality went without saying.

With a genial, "thank you," Sela collected both keys and left the man to savor his new-found wealth.

She hoped he wouldn't try to cash it too soon. A coin that old would undoubtedly draw unnecessary attention and they needed time to plan their next move.

The question of roommates was a no-brainer.

Sela gave Freya her key, offering to help move the groggy and barely responsive Jacob into their room.

Freya waved her off, determined to do it herself. "It's only right. I got him into this mess. I should be taking responsibility for my actions for once."

Sela smiled as she watched the pair hobble through the door.

Turning, Sela noticed the door to the adjoining room was standing wide open. She glanced down at her hand — the key had gone.

Swallowing a chuckle, she walked in to see Anna trying to determine which of the beds had a better view of the television.

Sela's priority was to choose the least disgusting, frowning at the realization they had both failed.

"Has Mommy's little pickpocket made a decision?" Sela chuckled, arching a brow.

"Sadly, *None of the Above* isn't an option," Anna moaned as she plumped on the bed closest to her. "This one is the least worst."

"*Least worst?* Who taught you English?" Sela ruffled her daughter's jet-black hair as she passed. "I promise the next place will be a five-star resort." Chortling when Anna swatted her hand away.

"You used to giggle when I did that when you were younger," Sela protested with motherly sorrow.

"Well, Mother, I'm no longer a child. I am almost at double digits, you know," Anna replied imperiously.

Their shared laughter sounded a trifle strained — they both knew the truth of Anna's words. She was not a child, never had been and, if her abilities at the campsite were any indicator, her magic had come into ascendency.

"You hungry?" Sela changed the subject, wanting to get out of the room.

"I could eat, but I thought the guy in the office was supposed to be bringing us something?" Anna was confused.

"He is, I'm not sure I can hold out that long. Besides, I'd like to explore our new surroundings and see what we can scavenge."

"You mean steal."

"Potato, *potahhto*." Sela applied the age-old rule of semantics.

Sela and Anna meandered around the quaint little town of Baker, which hugged its namesake lake.

Typical of similar settlements, scattered across the prairies, the majority of homes had been there since the town was founded, interspersed with a sprinkling of newer builds.

Mother and daughter chatted as they strolled along the lake, enjoying the mellow atmosphere, studiously avoiding any conversation relating to recent events.

They were impressed by the number of dining establishments for such a small town and, as they wandered along Main Street, came across one which also housed a casino.

Never one to miss an opportunity, Sela — after instructing her daughter not to talk to strangers, more for their safety than Anna's — ventured inside.

Dropping her last quarter in a slot, she curled her fingers around the coin wedged in her pocket.

She felt it warm her palm.

The word WINNER popped up on the display screen, accompanied by the peal of an annoyingly loud klaxon and the chink of coins spilling into the narrow metal tray.

Collecting the cache, she joined her daughter.

Anna, who had observed the whole thing through the glass frontage, admonished her mother when she came out, "For shame. Using magic like that."

"I have to feed you somehow, and you heard Freya, her purse is gone. I couldn't *borrow* a twenty from it now, could I?" Sela defended unrepentantly.

Anna's expression made her opinion on the matter quite plain as they wandered back along the street, spying a café on the corner. Filled with other patrons, it looked inviting.

The hostess greeted the pair with a warm smile and ushered them to a table by the window. Handing them a menu each, she said the waitress would take their order shortly.

Anna studied the options noting the place boasted a four-star review, which she pointed out to her mom. "This town must be a Mecca for foodies. The Casino had five, and pretty much every place we passed was the same. I wonder how bad a place has to be to get less."

"Maybe a meal in a motel room could stretch to three." Sela winked. "Now hush up and decide what you want."

Over burgers, fries, and shakes, the two were like any other mother and daughter — enjoying an afternoon together without a care in the world.

Sela would have preferred to be eating pizza in Central Park with Anna, but the café wasn't bad.

Munching the last of her mom's fries, Anna asked, "Do you have any idea where we are going?"

Sela sat back, watching her daughter devour her food; memories of the girl's father eating the same way crowded in.

"As much as Freya is against it, I'm still thinking New York City is our best bet. It's large enough to lose ourselves within. I'm sure we'll be safe there," Sela replied.

With no knowledge of New York, Anna could not comment either way.

Hiding from a host of Norse deities sucked; but doing so in a city her mother had been telling her about since the day she was born, might be better than sticking around this place.

"Sounds like a plan." Anna beamed her acquiescence.

Sela paid the bill and, rather than continue their tour of the place, the two retraced their steps to the motel.

Anna presumed she had dozed off watching television. The motel's satellite service was sketchy at best; half the time, a passing cloud killed the signal. Her assumption the repetitive on again, off again had lulled her to sleep proved erroneous when she realized she was not in the motel room.

Although familiar with out of body experiences, she was always the one to initiate them.

This time it was different. Someone had drawn her to this dark, dank cave.

She registered movement out of the corner of her eye. Slowly, Anna turned to see a massive serpent struggling to keep something clenched in its powerful jaws.

Its tortured gaze seemed to beg Anna for help.

At first, Anna could not understand what the creature was asking of her. That was until she saw the glint of a mighty axe fall, dismembering its tail, leaving bloody stump dangling in the serpent's teeth.

A tremendous roar filled the darkness and the cave began to crumble around her. The flicker of a torch illuminated the axe bearer, as he scrambled to escape.

It was her father, and she recognized where she was.

Anna woke up, drenched in sweat and screaming.

CHAPTER

FOURTEEN

Panicked shrieks shattered Sela's slumber.

Without thinking, she snatched one of her swords from its scabbard and sprang up, ready to attack.

Certain they had been discovered by the valkyries, she scanned the room for intruders.

The television screen cast the room in a ghostly hue. Squinting in the gloom, Sela heard wretched sobs, and scooted across to Anna's bed.

Ashen faced, sitting in a huddle, arms hooked around her legs and chin on her knees, Anna rocked back and forth, whimpering, "No. No. No."

Sela dropped her sword.

Perching on the edge of the mattress, she drew Anna into her embrace, brushing her forehead with a gentle kiss. Anna's rigid body went limp as Sela cradled the child waiting for her sobs to subside.

"We have to stop him," Anna hiccupped.

"Stop who, sweetheart? Who do we need to stop?"

"It's Dad. He's about to do something he shouldn't, but

I can't reach him. He didn't see me, Mom... why didn't he see me?" The words poured from Anna almost too fast for comprehension.

Tightening her hug, Sela whispered into her daughter's hair, "Shhh... it was just a bad dream. You said so yourself, your dad is somewhere beyond..."

"No, Mom, he's not." Anna flung herself out of her mother's arms to pace the room. "This is what I wanted to tell you at the campground, only..." she let that trail off, twisting her fingers together.

In a trembling voice she summoned up the courage to admit, "H-he is alive. He was being held captive in Helheim by my crazy half-sister. Evidently, D-dad somehow breached a barrier Hel had trapped him in. I don't know how... b-but now I can't reach him. I should be able to. I should be able to stop him."

Her pacing became frantic, the solution to this gargantuan problem eluding her.

Stunned by Anna's revelation, Sela remained motionless on her daughter's bed.

*Loki was... is... **alive?*** She could *not* get her head around it.

The shock rendered her temporarily insensible to everything else around her and she had no clue what else Anna was babbling about, until she saw the girl staring at her.

"Mom, what are we going to do?" Anna's question demanded Sela's answer.

"*Where* did you see your dad?" Sela fought to clear her head.

"He was in a cave. Not just any cave. It was Jörmungandr's lair," Anna said as though mere mention of the name was enough to convey the gravity of the situation.

It was.

Acquainted with the legend about Loki's mythical serpent son, who encircled the world, Sela always supposed it was naught but a folk tale, parents told their children to scare them about the end of existence — Norse child rearing at its best.

To discover it was true, terrified Sela.

"We have to stop him. If he is successful, it will be the end of everything," Anna pleaded, all but bouncing on her feet, willing her mother to move.

In a split second Sela had skirted the beds, and was opening the door to Freya's adjoining room without knocking.

No time for formalities.

"Freya, Anna says we need to leave right n—" Sela's words died in her throat at the scene which met her eyes.

A naked goddess riding a similarly naked ranch owner was more than Sela, than *anyone* needed to see.

She spun on her heel, hearing the rustle of bedclothes.

"Dammit, Sela," Freya barked as she yanked the comforter around her. "Perfect timing as usual. What do you want?"

Uncharacteristically embarrassed, Sela gave Freya the condensed version of what was about to happen.

She grasped Freya's arm, urging her into action, but the goddess didn't budge.

"I'm not going, Sela. I'm done." Freya glanced at Jacob. "I belong here," her words were soft and rang with conviction.

"Well that's all fine and dandy, but what will this," she gestured between the two, "matter if Loki implements what Anna saw?" Sela reproved bitterly, confused by Freya's attitude.

"Then I'll die with the man I love," Freya replied. "All

stories eventually come to an end, don't they? Maybe this is just my *Happily Ever After*."

Incredulous, Sela stared at her friend, unable to believe what she was hearing.

"Freya, how can you stand by without lifting a finger? It's not okay to let everyone die because you prefer to indulge in a grand romance."

Sela didn't see Freya move but, suddenly, her hands were clasped.

The two locked eyes for the briefest of moments before Sela felt the surge rush through her body.

The pair was engulfed in the purest of Nature's energy. It lifted them from the floor, suspending them in time and space.

Freya channeled everything she possessed into Sela.

As the last vestiges of the goddess's magic flowed out, Sela saw a smile of unmistakable relief light Freya's face, prompting Sela to kiss her on the cheek as they landed gently on the floor.

Freya wrapped her friend in a fierce hug, whispering into her ear, "Go save us."

FIFTEEN

L oki stood at the entrance to Jörmungandr's dismal world. As much as he hated the existence of this place, he hated himself more for siring this wretched creature.

Hel could complain about being banished to run Helheim all she wanted, it could never match the lifetime of solitude Jörmungandr endured.

Loki swore that Odin's injustice to his children would finally come to an end.

Confident his decision was for the best, Loki steeled his emotions. Maybe he would be happy back in his own dimension. It had been eons since he had been able to return for more than just an occasional visit.

Besides, he'd have Hel to keep him company... probably.

As for his son, Jörmungandr would be free of his misery.

"That's all that matters," he wasn't completely certain who he was trying to convince.

He struck out along the path leading to the Lair.

The structure was designed to prevent anyone, mortal

or not, from stumbling across the 'World Serpent' unwittingly. Only a select few were permitted entry.

The place was immense.

In order to hide its location, all of Earth's magic originated here, effectively concealing the cave's opening and anyone within.

The supernatural defenses radiating from this prison were so intense, they interfered with telepathic communication.

Should anyone happen to advance beyond the mouth of the cave, the path provided no safety, separating into multiple trails, each — save the correct one — winding sinuously into an endless abyss.

Death awaited those foolish enough to attempt the journey.

Even the walls were designed to impede successful navigation of the passage. Light was absorbed by the stone. The illumination provided by even the strongest of torches was scarcely more than a faint glimmer.

Without a sharp eye and a steady foot, the most intrepid of explorers would walk off the edge and plummet to their deaths, or were destined to remain lost forever on one of the labyrinthine trails.

The putrid odor of decay hung thickly over this place.

Loki arrived at the forks in the path before requiring his torch. He did not move until his vision had adapted to the blackness of the cave.

He sensed Hel next to him before she spoke, "What are you waiting for, Father? If you ever loved any of us, get moving and avenge us."

Holding his torch close to her face, Loki studied Hel, wordlessly. Dismissing the nagging yet, thus far, fleeting disquiet, he continued down the tortuous path to the heart of the Lair.

The deeper Loki went, the hotter the cave became. Jörmungandr's chamber lay within the Earth's magma, just above the core and, thankfully, too deep for even the longest man-made boring equipment.

As he approached the ancient door behind which Jörmungandr was locked, the stench of sulfur and melting rocks singed Loki's nostrils, the heat — unbearable.

Standing in front of the massive frame, Loki wiped his brow trying to stem the beads of sweat running down his face and burning his eyes, without success.

To make matters worse, Hel goaded him again.

"If you think it's hot here, Father dearest, try spending your life in Helheim. It's just as bad there. Open the door and let us get this over with."

"Bullshit, Hel. Compared with this, your realm has all the comforts of a Swiss ski resort... complete with indoor plumbing, no less."

Hel had no idea what her father was talking about, but masked her ignorance because it appeared important to him.

"A Swiss should be so lucky."

Attempting to regulate his increasing irascibility, Loki pinched the bridge of his nose.

Knowing his daughter would never concede that Jörmungandr's life had been far more miserable than hers, he switched to another topic requiring an answer.

"Given the stringent efforts devoted to hiding him, how *did* you find your brother?"

Her gigantic hand on her father's back, Hel urged him closer to the door.

He could hear hints of agitation in her voice as she

explained, "I have followed you numerous times to this place, but *here* is where you lose your nerve, where you once more abandoned another child."

Her irritation morphed into outright anger. "I don't have the magic to unlock this door. I can only stand here and listen to his sorrowful pleas for release through this enchanted wood, knowing there is nothing I can do for him.

"Open the damned door."

Shame was a relatively new emotion to Loki, and for Hel to exploit it to her advantage, fuelled his rapidly deteriorating temper.

Nevertheless, he shrugged her hand from his back to concentrate on the door.

Sweeping his hand over the darkened wood, Loki demanded it obey him and open. The door refused to comply. Loki repeated his order with the same result.

The door's defiance infuriated Loki.

His iron self-control slipped.

In a paroxysm of rage, he swung the formidable battle-axe he had carried down with him, and battered the door.

The African Blackwood, from which the door was constructed, temporarily held its own against the savagery of Loki's sudden attack. The timbers chipped and bowed inward under the assault of the finely honed axe head.

Another blow ruptured the door's seal. Shards of wood pelted Loki and Hel.

The barrage of splinters aside, now they were confronted by the festering miasma oozing through the gaping opening, noxious punishment for daring to trespass.

Despite spending her long existence contending with the reek of rotting flesh, this was almost too much for Hel.

Father and daughter shared a look.

Loki could not interpret Hel's expression, but when she

inclined her head, he, ignoring the vague niggle which pestered at the back of his mind, nodded and the two pushed on.

After what seemed like a never-ending descent, the tunnel widened into the Lair's antechamber, the enormity of which, while offering a marginal reprieve from the intolerable heat of the pathway, was impregnated by an acrid odor, so oppressive it clung to each breath Hel and Loki took.

The room was illuminated by the magma which surrounded the outer layer of the cavern, bathing the chamber in the dull reddish-orange of dying embers.

Loki's torch barely augmented the light. Its flame flickered against the walls which were covered in an ancient Norse containment spell.

It was meant to restrain and damn the soul within for eternity.

Loki examined the curse, his inspection diverted when he discovered crude, childlike drawings of a serpent interspersed among the writing.

A curious wave of melancholy assailed him; there could be only one author.

Hel tugged at his arm, steering him towards the last passage that led to Jörmungandr. The smell alone was enough of a guide, but the heavy breathing echoing throughout the main chamber affirmed their direction.

Loki frowned at the heavy, forged chains circling Jörmungandr's body. Each chain was secured to an equally thick stake driven hundreds of feet into the rock.

Even the slightest of movements from Jörmungandr brought the inhabitants of Earth far above massive earthquakes. His bonds made anything but a wriggle an impossibility.

Hel and Loki followed his body in search of his head... and tail. The beginning and end of Loki's blighted son, and of all life, lay in the same place.

Odin had cursed Jörmungandr with the responsibility of holding together the whole of existence by clutching his tail in his mouth.

The thought of destroying Odin for that deed alone brought a wicked smirk to Loki's face.

It did not take long to find what they were looking for.

Jörmungandr's gaze met Loki's.

There was no hint of surprise at seeing his father. He knew his sire would return to visit him, one day.

For the first time since being banished here, his features softened into the semblance of a smile.

His eyes fell on his father's companion, widening with fear when he recognized Hel. He hissed a warning to his father to flee... or kill her.

Oblivious to his son's terror, Loki patted Jörmungandr on the side of his head, "I'm happy to see you, too, my son. On my oath, this will all be over quickly."

Jörmungandr clamped his jaw more tightly around his tail. Pain coursed through his body, sending tremors around the planet. Droplets of blood stained his teeth as, desperately, he tried to prevent what was about to happen.

His wails became louder and more insistent.

His father *had* to realize the lie before it was too late.

SIXTEEN

T he mighty axe glinted when Loki raised it aloft.

Jörmungandr closed his eyes as he saw it fall. There was no chance of reaching his father, of changing his mind.

He waited for the end.

A small voice rang out, echoing around the chamber, **"Dad, no."**

With supreme effort, Loki hefted the axe sideways, burying the head into the stone next to Jörmungandr.

Sparks lit the Lair, silhouetting two figures running in his direction.

Loki gawked as the glittering dots died away.

"Leave me alone, **ghosts**," Loki roared. "Get out of my mind. I know you're dead."

"No, Loki," Sela injected a note of authority into her voice. It was crucial he believed they were real. "We are here to take you home."

"Please, Father. Listen to Mom. All my life you have been telling me that one day you would come for us, but it is our turn to save you."

"You don't exist. Neither of you. I saw you die in the park. You're just figments of my insanity, of my torment. I caused it..."

The axe slithered from Loki's grip as he slumped to the floor of the cavern.

This was a nightmare, a manifestation of his hope, distorted by his madness. He was still floundering in the chasm of his own grief.

Loki buried his face in hands and surrendered to his fate.

Two pairs of arms enveloped him, wrested him from his self-pity.

Confounded by the sensation, he looked up to see his wife and his daughter — his family.

They were *not* an illusion; they were real, flesh and blood, and they were here.

Inundated by a welter of emotions, he clutched them tightly to his body, breathing in their scent.

Realization smacked him between the eyes, his wrath mounted, and he glared at Hel.

"How could you lie...?" the rest of the accusation froze on Loki's lips as his daughter transformed into Odin before his appalled eyes.

Sadistic spite radiated off the Asgardian as he slow-clapped contemptuously.

"Awww... how sweet, quite the keepsake moment," he sneered. "A family reunited, this makes it so much easier to rid myself of the lot of you. I hope you accept your fate as gracefully as Hel. She seemed to embrace her demise. Then again, she always was a strange creature."

Odin rose over the huddled family. Once he had vanquished them, he could absorb their magic to push him over the dimensional barrier — of that he was certain.

He opened his hands and a flurry of lightning bolts erupted from his palms. The ground shook as Odin's hatred-fueled energy engulfed the trio.

As the onslaught faded, a hulking wolf catapulted itself at Odin, sinking its fangs into the god's leg, knocking him to the ground. Teeth gnashed on the flesh and bone clenched in its powerful jaws. Odin's blood dripped from the wolf's mouth.

He bellowed in pain, and kicked at the wolf. "***Release me, Loki. I command you.***"

A lucky boot caught the side of Loki's head, and the wolf tumbled across the stone. Shifting, he snatched the axe and spun around to face Odin, only to find him gone.

Thunderously mocking laughter captured Loki's attention, and he raised his eyes to the roof of the cave.

"Come down here, coward, and let's end this," Loki bawled.

Odin's reply, a hailstorm of energy.

Loki readied himself for the punishing fury, only to have his feet knocked out from under him by a slender body. He reeled across the floor like a drunkard, and fell flat on his back. Winded, he blinked, his gaze landing on Sela's delicate countenance.

"Must I save your cute butt every time, *ástin mín*?" She smiled at him. Being able to call Loki *my love* again, fueled her determination to end Odin. Brushing a kiss to his lips, she planted the palms of her hands on his chest and pushed herself upright.

Loki was surprised — although why eluded him, this was Sela after all — when her swords materialized in her hands. *Wait... no...* awe supplanted surprise as he registered it was more than that; her hands had actually *become* the swords.

He intended to ask her *how* she managed that trick, but this was not the time.

He followed his wife, and the pair confronted Odin. Savagely, Sela slashed at the Asgardian's face; one of her blades slicing his left ear from his head.

"You two are the bane of my existence," Odin sneered and, seizing Sela as though she was nothing but a ragdoll, threw her at Loki. "Your deaths will be like sunlight after the storm."

The couple toppled to the ground, jarring Jörmungandr's head.

The impact of their combined weight caused the serpent's grip on his tail to falter. He struggled to maintain his grasp, deepening his bite. His body arched violently against the chains, sending powerful shockwaves through the Earth's crust.

Spying cracks developing in the stone cavern, Odin concocted a new battle plan.

Ignoring Loki and Sela, he switched his attack to the World Serpent, concentrating his energy on the gaping wound at Jörmungandr's tail. He doubled his efforts when he saw the flesh begin to cleave in two.

Without warning, Odin felt himself being yanked from the air. Arms cartwheeling, he could not stop his downwards plunge and slammed onto the stone floor.

Heaving himself to his feet, he soared again, only to suffer a repeat performance.

Slow to rise this time, his infuriated gaze sought out Sela and Loki, preparing to destroy them both for daring to assault him, baffled to see the pair preoccupied with trying to save the mangled remains of Jörmungandr's tail.

That was when his attention darted to the diminutive,

glowing figure in front of him. Red eyes, brimming with loathing, stared down the All Father.

"I think you will discover the bane of your sorry existence is me," Anna's pure bell-like tones, in stark contrast with the venom emanating from her prey.

"Nature and Magic have judged you guilty of abusing your gifts, Odin of Asgard," she pronounced judgment in the most ancient of tongues.

"There will be no mercy for you, Old Man. Your death will be complete, and your existence will be wiped from memory."

"No." Terror clawed at Odin upon hearing the sentence. He spluttered objections and threatened, "How dare you speak to me with such blatant disrespect, girl.

"I am Odin of Asgard. I am all magic.

"A pitiful creature such as you cannot possibly possess the power to destroy me. No one does. Your pathetic family will never know peace."

Incandescent with rage, Odin summoned all his power, and cast it at the insolent brat, satisfied when Anna vanished in a towering shroud of energy.

Rising to his feet, he prepared to rid the realms of her parents as well.

"Is that the best you have, Asgardian?" The angry voice boomed from within the stormy mass.

Stupefied, Odin watched the girl absorb the blast and emerge unscathed. He scrambled to bombard her with another volley.

Too late.

Anna stretched her arms out in front of her and clenched her hands together in a death grip.

Odin glanced down at his sides, feeling his arms being crushed under a tremendous invisible pressure.

Convinced Anna had summoned creatures from whatever pit of Helheim, she had crawled out of, he was appalled to realize it was the child herself who controlled his fate.

Reduced to begging for his life, Odin screeched a painful pledge, "I-I believe in your strength, girl. Spare me and I will grant you anything you want, untold wealth, dominion over all realms but Asgard."

Closing her eyes, Anna silenced his shrieks.

Slowly, her eyes opened and focused on his chest. "Your immortality has been rescinded by your malfeasance."

Her proclamation echoed with a strange dissonance, at odds with her usual melodic tones.

Odin, the All-Father, once the most honorable, the most noble, and the most wise was doomed.

"Was it worth it?"

Giving him no chance to reply, Anna drew in a long breath, inhaling the immortal magic from his body then, lifting her arms, hurled the malevolent god upwards.

Helpless, Odin was propelled towards the unforgiving stone ceiling of the cavern. He tried to fight the swift ascent, to no avail — Anna's power was too strong.

Odin crashed into the craggy roof. His neck snapped upon impact, and his body went limp. Anna forced him through the crevice, which shredded his flesh as he was ground against the jagged edges, and pitched him into the magma.

The fires of Earth consumed the once mighty god, instantly.

Anna watched the molten rock fill the hole left by Odin's body. A few drops of sizzling magma fell to the cavern floor, immediately solidifying into a single chunk of obsidian streaked with a rare and almost neon blue.

"Who's pitiful now?" she asked the fetid air pertly. Bending, she picked up the stone and shoved it in her pocket before running to join her parents.

Feverishly, Loki and Sela were trying to staunch the blood gushing from Jörmungandr's tail. The bone had been severed, leaving only tendons holding the massive appendage in place.

The tremors caused by his pain threatened not only to rupture the remains of his tail, but also Earth.

Boulders crashed from the ceiling, narrowly missing the couple, but peppering Jörmungandr's tormented body.

"There's no time," Loki yelled to Sela, "We have to jump now."

"We both know what will happen to me in your dimension," Sela countered. "Take Anna and save yourselves. I'll stay here with Jörmungandr as long as possible. *Now, go…*"

"No, Sela. I lost you once and cannot let that happen again. We can figure this out on the other side."

Both parents stopped when they felt a small hand slip into one of theirs. A warm, unidentifiable energy passed through them and into Jörmungandr's wound. Bone and flesh began to knit together as the three pulled tighter.

Jörmungandr's tormented writhing lessened, as did the quakes. No longer ravaged by pain, he was able to relax somewhat.

Anna opened one eye to peek at her half-brother. A smile came to her face as she informed him through her mind that she would visit him… a lot.

Exhausted, he managed a broad snaggle-toothed smile and winked back, happy not to be alone anymore.

"We will figure out how to free you of this curse," Loki assured his son.

Jörmungandr knew there was no reversing the enchantment, but it mattered not. He had family.

EPILOGUE

T he aftermath of the harrowing events was like an out of body experience for the five affected.

The rest of the world remained blissfully ignorant of how close they had come to disaster and, other than some damage caused by earthquakes... not an unusual occurrence... life continued without so much as a blink.

The tranquility of Wise River... repairs well underway... became a haven where grief was assuaged, injuries healed, and love avowed.

Jacob refused to wait any longer to marry his adored Freya, declaring she clearly required a stabilizing influence, which earned him a sharp elbow to the ribs.

Determined to keep his new family close — Anna still had a lot to learn about hunting — Jacob had designed an addition to the homestead. A second house, completely detached, but linked to the main building by a raised wooden walkway spanning the gap between the respective, wrap-around porches.

While astounded the man still wanted them around, all things considered, Sela and Loki had been touched by his generosity and accepted the offer gladly.

An arrangement which suited everyone.

Outwardly, Anna was a chirpy and typically insouciant soon-to-be nine-year-old, happy to be living next door to her adopted grandfather.

Inwardly, she was ageless, her power incalculable, which made for some hilarious... and occasionally hairy... interludes.

Loki and Sela spent hours out in the fields.

Sometimes, they talked — Loki, especially, needed to verbalize the impact of Hel's death, and his guilt in not heeding the warning which had pestered his subconscious.

"I am still confounded at the lengths Odin was prepared to go to destroy all the realms, to the extent of inhabiting my daughter's body to deceive me. *Me*, the Trickster God! Where's the logic?" he said to Sela one afternoon when they were trying to make sense of the lunacy.

"There is no logic once madness has taken over, only chaos. What's the saying? If I can't have it, no one can. Odin's power and his reason were so intertwined that when he lost one, the other was shattered," Sela posited.

"Plus, he knew how to play on your one weakness, your loved ones. He knew you would never give up on Hel, despite how obnoxious she was."

Loki conceded her point and, in the end, revisiting it

would not change the result. He had to find a way to accept and let go.

Sometimes, they walked in silence, savoring time alone together.

Sometimes, they argued — inevitable, given their fiery personalities, and which usually ended with Loki kissing Sela into dizzy delirium.

Precious moments rekindling what they thought lost forever.

Life moved on.

Three Months Later

In the confines of the vestry of Wise River's tiny chapel, a former goddess was being helped into her wedding finery.

The dress — a pale tan, deerskin hide, and all the more special because it was the result of Jacob and Anna's hunting prowess — was so soft it felt like silk.

Cleverly cut, it hugged Freya's shapely figure, flaring ever-so slightly from her hips to her knees, and falling gently to the floor in a deep fringe.

Hand-stitched by some of the elder-women from the Reservation, it was decorated with exquisite traditional and symbolic Crow beadwork. Closer examination of the patterns across the bodice revealed the Norse runes for Love, Luck, and Life.

"You have to take it back," Sela pleaded.

"There's only one thing I *have* to do, and we're going to be late if you don't stop complaining. I don't want Jacob thinking I'm absconding again."

Freya winked at her Maid of Honor's reflection in the mirror, blissfully unaware her groom, determined the ceremony would indeed go off without a hitch this time, had placed extra ushers by the doors and flattened the tires on his wife-to-be's brand new Cougar.

She flapped the delicate leather ribbons which cinched her slender waist. "Please tie these."

Doing as she was bidden did not divert Sela from coaxing Freya into reclaiming her magic.

"There is too much power for me to control. Yesterday, I was writing down the ingredients for Irish stew, and ended up in some bar in Dublin. Sean the Bartender sends his regards, by the way... *and* he gave me his grandmother's recipe."

Freya chuckled. "Wow, you must have made an impression. I hope he offered you a pint of Guinness, truly an elixir of the Gods."

"More likely, he wanted rid of me before his customers realised I'd materialized out of thin air." Sela stepped back to admire the bride.

Tweaking the gown, here and there, Freya gave her final decision on the topic, "Sorry, doll, there is no way I'm going through that again. No more goddess headaches for me. It took me too many lifetimes to find somebody worthy... or foolish... enough to pass it on to.

"Besides, you don't want to be left defenseless and at the mercy of your family, do you?"

Freya's brow furrowed. "Speaking of which, where is your lug of a husband. I can't be giving myself away now can I?"

Sela brushed a kiss to Freya's cheek and smiled. "If I know the boys, they're probably having one last celebratory toast before the ceremony."

"He damn well better not have Jack pie-eyed again. It took everything I had to get him out of bed after the bachelor party," Freya grumbled.

On cue, there was a knock on the door, and an extremely dapper-looking Loki strolled in.

Bowing, he announced, "It is time, Fair Ladies."

Loki kissed Sela, and swatted her butt playfully. Sela rolled her eyes at her husband, but could not prevent the loving smile which curved her lips.

He exclaimed to Freya, "May I say what a beautiful bride you are, Freya."

Freya blushed as she walked to the sanctuary entrance. Waiting for him to join her, she joked, "Lucky for you, I was fully clothed before you barged in."

Taking his place next to Freya, Loki hooked her slender arm around his huge one and pecked her on the cheek. Patting her hand he smirked. "I knew you were dressed. I've been peeking through the keyhole the whole time.

"Let's get you married."

After a day of joyful celebration, all was quiet.
The bride and groom had left, as had the guests.
The night air was cool.

Above, the moon was beginning its time-honored journey across a crystal-clear sky, surrounded by a gossamer blanket of twinkling stars.

Sitting on the swing chair on the newly completed porch of the homestead, Loki and Sela were chatting about the day, sipping steaming coffee. Anna had excused herself claiming she was tired, unaware her doting parents knew this was a euphemism for, 'I need to watch television.'

Jacob and Freya's wedding had been proclaimed the event of the decade by all and sundry, as they waved the happy couple off on their honeymoon — destination undisclosed.

"You do realize, we ought to go home at some point." Loki looked at his wife. He had 'checked' on their apartment, but was strangely reluctant to return to the cacophony that was Manhattan.

It was as though Sela had read his mind. "I know but, and I never thought I'd say this, although I love New York, this place has wormed its way into my heart."

"Bit like I did?" Loki teased.

Sela snuggled against him, relishing the weight of his arm around her shoulders, holding her close. A sensation she thought never to feel again. "Hmmm..." she opened her hands, palms up, and mimicked a set of scales out of balance. "You, or Wise River... you or Wise River..."

"Minx." He chuckled and curbed her nonsense with a searing kiss.

Death metal blared from Anna's room, shattering the stillness. The couple broke apart laughing.

"I see she's inherited your taste for that ear-splitting racket." Loki shook his head. He never understood how his wife found this so-called music, soothing... *soothing*...? "She ought to have played it to Odin... one bar of that would have finished him off without a drop of blood being spilled."

He looked at Sela, unwilling to articulate the gnawing concern at the back of his mind. Not today, not after so much happiness.

Sela caught and interpreted his expression immediately.

She pressed a gentle finger to his lips. "Don't say it, *ástin mín*. I know this might not be over, but it is for now. We'll cross that bridge when we come to it... *if* we come to it. I think we deserve a bit of peace and quiet for a while, don't you?"

Winking impishly, she nodded towards the house. "Remember, we have the advantage... Odin's Bane in there has it covered."

About the Author
RORI BLEU

With a smattering of riverboat pirates and royalty in her heritage, Rori Bleu's childhood reflected her past.
An interest in fairy tales, myth and legend were as important as spirited discussions around politics and current affairs — although some might argue they are one and the same!

A fascination, sparked by listening to Grimm's Fairy Tales at her grandmother's knee, not only encouraged Rori's passion for reading, but also steered her into the world of RPG's.
What began as a fun pastime, soon evolved into the creation of fantastical worlds, but Rori never lost her love of politics going on to specialise in Governmental History and Historical Research.

Naturally this means her stories are steeped in historical accuracy and real-life intrigue. While Rori's love of a happily ever after means her preferred genre is romance, don't be surprised if you discover an occasional detour into historical fiction, thrillers, horror and fantasy.

To find more of Rori's books... click the link
https://linktr.ee/roribleu

About the Author

ROSIE CHAPEL

Rosie Chapel lives in Perth, Australia with her hubby and two furkids. When not writing, she loves catching up with friends, burying herself in a book (or three), discovering the wonders of Western Australia, or — and the best — a quiet evening at home with her husband, enjoying a glass of wine and a movie.

Website: www.rosiechapel.com

Also by Rori Bleu

Pineapple Meringue

Imprisoned Hearts

Port of London

Dani's Masquerade

Black Tulips

Ajei's Destiny

Porta Aeternum

The Queen's Heart

Syn *with Matthew Forester*

Echoes and Illusions *with Rosie Chapel*

Evie's War *with Rosie Chapel*

Vindicta *with Rosie Chapel*

The Sela Helsdatter Saga *with Rosie Chapel*

A Flip of The Coin - Book One

Conceived Chaos - Book Two

Also by Rosie Chapel

Once Upon An Earl - Book One

To Unlock Her Heart - Book Two

Love on a Winter's Tide - Book Three

A Love Unquenchable - Book Four

A Hidden Rose — Book Five

The Daffodil Garden

The Unconventional Duchess

Rescuing Her Knight - *the de Wiltons:* Book One

Elusive Hearts - *An Unexpected Romance*: Book One

His Fiery Hoyden

A Regency Duet

A Regency Christmas Double

Fate is Curious

A Christmas Prayer *with Ashlee Shades*

The Lady's Wager

Winning Emma

A Love Impossible

Unravelling Roana

Love Kindled

Moonbeams and Mistletoe

Fairy Tale Romance

Chasing Bluebells

Contemporary Romances

Of Ruins and Romance

All At Once It's You

Cobweb Dreams

Just One Step

His Heart's Second Sigh

<u>Dystopian Romance</u>

Echoes & Illusions *with Rori Bleu*